DEATH TIMES THREE

BITTER END
FRAME-UP FOR MURDER
ASSAULT ON A BROWNSTONE

"Each piece in this volume is carefully wrought, each is from a period when Stout was in top writing form, each contains incomparable moments, insights, and sallies of wit that will take their place in the memories of devotees of the saga."—from the Introduction by John McAleer

REX STOUT'S
NERO WOLFE

"It is always a treat to read a Nero Wolfe mystery. The man has entered our folklore; he is part of the psyche of anybody who has ever turned over the pages of a mystery novel. Like Sherlock Holmes . . . he looms larger than life and, in some ways, is much more satisfactory."
—*The New York Times Book Review*

"Nero Wolfe is one of the master creations."
—James M. Cain, author of *The Postman Always Rings Twice*

"The most interesting great detective of them all."
—Kingsley Amis, author of *Lucky Jim*

"This fellow is the best of them all."
—Supreme Court Justice Oliver Wendell Holmes

Death Times Three
Rex Stout

A Nero Wolfe Mystery

**With an Introduction
by
John J. McAleer**

BANTAM BOOKS
TORONTO · NEW YORK · LONDON · SYDNEY · AUCKLAND

DEATH TIMES THREE

A Bantam Book / December 1985

PRINTING HISTORY

"Bitter End" first appeared in the November 1940 issue of
The American Magazine, *and later in a limited edition volume*
entitled CORSAGE.

"Frame-Up for Murder" originally appeared in the June 21st,
June 28th, and July 5, 1958 editions of The Saturday Evening
Post.

"Assault on a Brownstone" appeared in substantially differ-
ent form as "The Counterfeiter's Knife" in the January 14th,
January 21st, January 28th issues of The Saturday Evening
Post *in 1961, and as "Counterfeit for Murder" in* HOMICIDE
TRINITY.

ISBN 0-553-25425-1

Published simultaneously in the United States and Canada

Bantam Books are published by Bantam Books, Inc. Its trade-
mark, consisting of the words "Bantam Books" and the por-
trayal of a rooster, is Registered in U.S. Patent and Trademark
Office and in other countries. Marca Registrada. Bantam
Books, Inc., 666 Fifth Avenue, New York, New York 10103.

PRINTED IN THE UNITED STATES OF AMERICA

H   0 9 8 7 6 5 4 3 2 1

Contents

Introduction

During the last years of Rex Stout's life, as his author-
ized biographer, I received numerous letters from well-
wishers and, on occasion, not-such–well-wishers, offering
me advice. "Is it true," one of the latter asked, "that
Stout has a secretary who writes all his stuff for him?" I
showed the letter to Rex, then in his eighty-ninth year.
He scanned it and said, "Tell him the name is Jane
Austen, but I haven't the address." The joke was on the
letter writer. Rex was classing himself with the best.
Not long before that he had told me, "I used to think
that men did everything better than women, but that
was before I read Jane Austen. I don't think any man
ever wrote better than Jane Austen."

It was no coincidence that, when I asked after
Wolfe a few days before Rex died, Rex confided, "He's
rereading *Emma*." Rex ranked *Emma* as Jane Austen's
masterpiece. In the last weeks of his life he also reread
it. That a book could be reread was to him solid proof of
its worth. Thus it pleased him when P. G. Wodehouse,
whom Rex admired, declared, at ninety-four, in a letter

that he wrote to me, "He [Rex Stout] passes the supreme test of being rereadable. I don't know how many times I have reread the Nero Wolfe stories, but plenty. I know exactly what is coming and how it is all going to end, but it doesn't matter. That's *writing*."

Since Rex's death, on October 27, 1975, the radiant host that constitutes his loyal following has reread many times the thirty-three novels and thirty-eight novellas believed to make up the entire corpus of the Wolfe saga. How jubilant must be this worldwide audience to learn now that many new pages of reading pleasure await it—a thirty-ninth novella, "Bitter End," known only to a smattering of readers; "Frame-up for Murder," a substantially expanded rewrite of "Murder Is No Joke," the existence of which has gone unsuspected by most Stout readers since it has never before appeared in book form; and a fortieth novella, the original version of "Counterfeit for Murder," which, after the first seven pages, pursues a plot line that differs markedly from that followed in the version eventually published in *Homicide Trinity* (1962). The existence of this unpublished manuscript was unknown, even to members of Rex Stout's own family, until 1972, when Rex furnished me a handwritten copy of his personal "Writing Record," in which the facts relating to its composition were recorded. A diligent search among his voluminous papers, at Boston College's Baptist Library, when they were delivered to the college following his death, disclosed that, contrary to his remembrance, he had not destroyed this manuscript and that there was, therefore, a seventy-third Nero Wolfe story that had never seen print. This discovery surpasses in significance the publication—in 1951, for the first time in the United States—of the fifty-first Father Brown story, "The Vampire of the Village," and the publication—in 1972, for the first time anywhere—of "Talboys," a hitherto unknown Lord Peter Wimsey story; it is on a par only with the discovery of an eightieth Sherlock Holmes story—an event which has not yet occurred.

For admirers of Nero Wolfe and Archie Goodwin, in the years between 1934 and 1975, the advent of a new Nero Wolfe story was ever an occasion for rejoicing. However, because the stories appeared with unfailing regularity (save for the years of World War II, when Rex Stout was heading up America's propaganda effort as chairman of the Writers' War Board), the thrill probably came to be regarded by many as theirs by right of entitlement. For a bona fide new story to come to light, after every legitimate hope for such an event had been relinquished, constitutes an occasion that must set the firmament ablaze with pyrotechnical wonders. What a windfall! What a gift from the stars! Yet, here we have, in this single volume, not only such a treasure, but two other Nero Wolfe tales largely new to us. None of the three, moreover, can be dismissed as a mere practice exercise, sketched out and flung aside by Rex Stout as beneath his standards. Each piece is carefully wrought; each is from a period when he was in top writing form; each contains incomparable moments, insights, and sallies of wit that will take their place in the memories of votaries of the corpus as new pinnacles in a landscape already wondrously sown with pinnacles. Let us consider each in its turn.

"Bitter End," published in *The American Magazine* in November 1940, was the first of what we now know to be forty Nero Wolfe novellas. But it began life not as a Nero Wolfe novella but as a Tecumseh Fox novel. In 1939, to accommodate his publishers, who had asked him to create another detective to spell Wolfe, Rex introduced Tecumseh Fox in *Double for Death*. Fox was not the superman Wolfe was, nor did he have

Archie's panache, but he did have brains and muscle and, without the advantage of a dogsbody to assist him, he worked out the solution to an intricate case. Rex's friends thought Fox was rather like Rex himself. Certainly, like Rex, he was on the move a lot. That was inevitable. Rex said he had made Wolfe housebound because other people's detectives "ran around too damn much." Yet he realized that two sedentary detectives would be too limiting.

In the summer of 1940 Rex was ready with a second Fox novel—*Bad for Business*. Farrar & Rinehart scheduled it for publication in November of that year in its *Second Mystery Book*, where it was to be the culminating tale in a volume that would include stories by Anthony Abbot, Philip Wylie, Leslie Ford, Mary Roberts Rinehart, and David Frome (a Leslie Ford alias) —*Bad for Business* though, weighing in at two hundred and five pages, was far and away the longest. As was customary, the story was offered to *The American Magazine* for abridged publication before the book itself appeared. To Stout's surprise, Sumner Blossom, publisher of *The American Magazine*, refused to pursue the Fox piece but offered Stout double payment if he would convert the story into a Wolfe novella. To Blossom's surprise, and maybe his own, Rex effected the transformation in eleven days. As he explained to me later, by then he had already become deeply committed to the war against Hitler and needed the money.

Thus "Bitter End," Rex's first Wolfe novella, appeared in *The American Magazine* in November 1940— and on November 28, *Bad for Business* appeared in the *Second Mystery Book*. Those who read both stories at that time must have been perplexed. The plot was basically unchanged. The names of the principal characters likewise were the same. This was true as well of many lines of dialogue and of many crucial expository passages. Yet, Tecumseh Fox's labors had been portioned out between Wolfe and Archie; Fox's nemesis from Homicide, Inspector Damon, had been supplanted, inevitably, by Inspector Cramer; and Dol Booner, whose path occasionally crossed Fox's in *Bad for Business,* had been dispensed with entirely.

These changes were by no means matter-of-fact substitutions. Although the new story was only a third as long as the original, compactness actually gave it a snap and purpose that it lacked before. Most of the members of the supporting cast were enhanced. They were not on stage as long as they had been before, so the moment an opportunity came their way, they made their presence felt. By dividing Fox's responsibilities between Wolfe and Archie, Rex showed how incomparable and how indispensable were the distinctive attributes of each member of his sublime duo. Each does superbly what Fox was able to do merely adequately. Working once again with the characters he loved best, Rex found ways to involve them intimately in events as they unfolded.

In *Bad for Business,* Tecumseh Fox learns secondhand that someone (in a prefiguration of the Tylenol tragedy of later times) is adulterating, apparently with sinister intent, Tingley's Tidbits, a liver paté. In "Bitter End," Nero Wolfe actually partakes of the paté, which is laced with quinine, and all but explodes at the dinner table, splattering a landscape that includes Archie. Predictably, and reminiscent of his duel to the death with Arnold Zeck, he commits himself to seeking out and revenging himself on the adulterator. Furthermore, Cramer abducts a guest from Wolfe's brownstone, simultaneously giving new scope to Wolfe's vendetta and a scope to Cramer's own performance that, by contrast, diminishes Inspector Damon's role. In *Bad for Business,* Tecumseh Fox learns secondhand of a bloody murder.

In "Bitter End," Archie arrives on the murder scene as one of the first witnesses. Surprisingly, though Fox openly romances the heroine in *Bad for Business*, in "Bitter End," Archie, though solicitous, keeps his distance. This enables Archie to give needed support to Amy's true suitor, the inept Leonard Cliff.

The viewpoint in *Bad for Business* is that of the omniscient author. In "Bitter End," naturally, Archie is the narrator. Rex Stout had proven that he could bring startling piquancy to a plot by relinquishing control of it to Archie, and we must concede that Stout showed excellent judgment in letting Archie be his spokesman throughout the Wolfe saga. When "Archie took control of the narrative," he said, he himself was no longer responsible for what Archie said and did. And he meant it. So successful were the results in "Bitter End" that we must regret that Rex was never motivated to rewrite each of the Fox stories as Wolfe stories, with Archie narrating. Let those who may undertake to continue the saga not leave that avenue unexplored. In "Bitter End," Rex Stout showed that it can be done with complete success.

It was not by chance that *Bad for Business* was never given separate hardcover publication in the United States or that Rex Stout dropped Fox after a few appearances. "Fox wasn't a created character, like Wolfe," Rex conceded. "He was put together piece-by-piece and wasn't worth a damn." Nonetheless, Fox's precedence as the sleuth who unknotted the tangled Tingley fortunes (in *Bad for Business*) made Rex reluctant to include "Bitter End" in his volumes of Wolfe novellas. Stout never went back and reread the story because he could not forget that Wolfe had been called in on the case as someone from whom a second opinion was sought. It was not becoming to Wolfe's dignity to sit him down to another man's leavings.

Rex ought to have remembered that a good story always stands the test of rereading. And "Bitter End," like the other seventy-two stories in the corpus, passes that test beyond quibble or sneer. Perhaps if Rex had remembered that it was this story that had shown him that Wolfe and Archie could thrive in a novella quite as well as in a novel, he would have given it due acknowledgment. Actually, in the last year of his life he may have come to that realization when he gave Michael Bourne permission to bring the story out in a limited edition of five hundred copies. Bourne conceived of this edition as a tribute to mark, in 1976, Rex's ninetieth birthday. Plans for it were still afoot when Rex died. In 1977, it appeared instead in the volume called *Corsage,* as a memorial tribute. Although its publication brought joy to those who were aware of it, the restriction Rex had placed on the number of copies to be printed resulted in a volume known to few readers who were not avid bibliophiles.

The entry in Rex Stout's Writing Record for "Murder Is No Joke," appears between the entries for *If Death Ever Slept* and *Champagne for One*. It reads: "Murder Is No Joke"—48 pp. Began 8/5/57, finished 8/15/57. 1 day out, 10 days writing time." Rex's breakdown, reporting his day by day output, shows that he worked on the story on eleven different days but counted two days as half days because he did not put in a full nine hours at his desk. On the thirteenth he had been interrupted by the arrival of a visitor. On the fifteenth he quit early because half a day's work brought him to the end of his labors. As usual, of course, he did no revision. Whatever had to be done was always done in his head. The first draft was always the only draft. "Murder Is No Joke" was the fourth story Rex worked on that year, because, in addition to *If Death Ever*

Slept, which he had begun in mid-May and finished in mid-June, he had finished "Easter Parade" in the first days of the new year, and then in March, in nine days, had written "Fourth-of-July Picnic." All were Nero Wolfe stories. Indeed, after World War II he wrote nothing else.

Notations in Rex's file on "Murder Is No Joke" disclose further writing labors for that year that were not entered in the Writing Record. On November 23, to oblige *The Saturday Evening Post*, he began work on an expanded version of "Murder Is No Joke." Taking only two days off, Sunday the twenty-fourth and Saturday the thirtieth, to celebrate his seventy-first birthday (when family and friends gathered at High Meadow, his eighteen-acre domain at Danbury, Connecticut), he completed the rewrite in thirteen days, having increased the original forty-eight pages to seventy-nine. Characteristically (Rex found holidays disruptive and, within reasonable limits, preferred to ignore them), he had written five pages on Thanksgiving Day and four on his birthday. Typically, also, he had not merely padded the old manuscript. He had thought the story through again, adding much that was new and enhancing what he kept. Now two different versions of the story existed, the latter clearly the superior of the former. Since that fact was self-evident, it should logically have followed that the original was suppressed in favor of the rewrite.

Yet that is not what happened. On February 14, 1958, as "Murder Is No Joke," the original was published in *And Four to Go*. On June 21, June 28, and July 5, 1958, as "Frame-up for Murder," the rewrite was published in three installments in the *The Saturday Evening Post*. Those who owned the book probably never compared their version to the *Post*'s version. Those who read the *Post*'s version probably never compared it to the version in *And Four to Go*. Thus no one complained that thirty-one pages of vintage Stout were buried in back issues of *The Saturday Evening Post*. But they were, and that was deplorable. Here, after a twenty-eight-year delay, as "Frame-up for Murder" achieves publication in book form another injustice is swept away.

In the notes that Rex Stout kept for this story—as always, on 5½ by 8½ goldenrod sheets—he recorded the following facts about eight of the characters: "Alec Gallant, 38, of Gallant Inc., 54th St. East of 5th. Bianca Voss, 37, who has taken charge. Carl Drew, 40, business manager & buyer. Anita Prince, 34, designer & fitter. Emmy Thorne, 26, contacts & promotion. Flora Gallant, 26, Alec's sister & handy woman. Sarah Yare, 35, has-been actress. Doris Hoft, 29, at phone." To readers of either version of the story the name Doris Hoft will come as a surprise. While Doris does have a small part to play in both versions, in neither does Rex mention her by name. More surprising to readers of "Murder Is No Joke" must be the revelation that Flora Gallant is twenty-six. In that story we are assured that she was twenty-five when she came to the United States from France, twenty years earlier, in 1937, and thus is forty-five. Rex's initial description of Flora bears this out. Archie relates, "When I opened the door to admit his sister Flora that Tuesday morning, it was a letdown to see a dumpy middle-aged female in a dark gray suit that was anything but spectacular. It needed pressing, and the shoulders were too tight, and her waist wasn't where it thought it was." In short, Flora is a frump who has seen her best days and these not lately. Nor does the ensuing dialogue encourage us to mellow toward her. She seems to be a bitter, spent woman who has outlived whatever romantic feelings she once had. With clinical detachment she dismisses the possibility of Wolfe's having a mistress, almost as one might rule out

the likelihood of his catching whooping cough or break-
ing out in pubescent acne. We resent this woman who
addresses Wolfe as though she were a case-hardened
clinician talking to a eunuch. And Flora is similarly
dispassionate when she says of brother Alec, " 'He has
an *amie intime*, a young woman who is of importance in
his establishment.' " The name Flora Gallant has en-
couraged us to expect something more. In "Murder Is
No Joke" Flora is no flower. She is more of a nettle.
That fact serves at least one good purpose. It makes it
easy to believe that she is capable of skulduggery or
even murder.

In "Frame-up for Murder" we must begin all over
with Flora. She first catches Archie's eye in the lobby of
the Churchill "because she rated a glance as a matter of
principle—the principle that a man owes it to his eyes
to let them rest on attractive objects when there are
any around." Her chin was, Archie acknowledged,
"slightly more pointed than I would have specified if I
had had her made to order," but otherwise her ranking
is high among the women who have intrigued Archie
Goodwin over the years. A shoulder spread of mink, a
floppy-brimmed hat, which is at Archie's ear level—so
that, as he notes, her hair might graze his chin if she
removed it—and a trace of a beguiling foreign accent,
are all that this Flora needs, in addition to her beauty,
to intrigue Archie. When she accosts him on the uptown side of Thirty-eighth Street, he confesses, "If she
had been something commonplace like a glamorous
movie star," he might have gone on his way without
further interest. But that does not happen. Flora's game
is to get to know Archie so that he will gain her an
audience with Nero Wolfe. She dines with him and
dances with him to assure the success of this strategem.
Her kisses are prologue to inquisitions. Yet, she is
naively obvious in her intrigues, and Archie, never for a

moment taken in, finds her simple, obvious machinations (embarked on for no more sinister a purpose than to protect her brother and his business) a source of unmitigated delight. This new Flora burgeons in the opening pages of "Frame-up for Murder." Her subsequent pursuit of Archie through the streets of Manhattan and her success in bringing him down, on the wing, so to speak, stirs our interest in a way that totally eclipses the opening of "Murder Is No Joke."

Rex Stout enjoyed portraying beautiful foreign women of fierce integrity whose hearts are set on realizing some laudable goal that they pursue with a tenacity that gives consequence to their obvious ploys when they try to enlist the services of those who can get them the results they want. In his beautiful wife, the Polish-born Pola Hoffman, their friends recognized the prototype of these women. Here, in a story set in the world of high fashion, the identification is more easily made, for Pola Stout was one of America's foremost designers of woolen fabrics and her fabrics were much in favor with top fashion houses both in the United States and Europe. It was Pola's calling that gave Rex the setting and plot for several other stories, most notably *The Red Box* and *Red Threads*, and made him always attentive to the clothes his characters were wearing.

In "Murder Is No Joke," Flora Gallant offers Nero Wolfe a hundred dollars as a retainer. In "Frame-up for Murder," as befits her upgraded status, the sum increases to three hundred, still not a princely offering from someone swathed in mink, but enough, Archie says, either to pay his salary for two days or to keep Wolfe in beer for three weeks. That Archie has mellowed toward Flora since her transformation from frog to princess is evident. In "Murder Is No Joke" he had calculated that her hundred-dollar deposit would, at most, buy beer for Wolfe for four days. But more than pecuniary advantages attach to Flora's new appearance. Her metamorphosis generated most of the new pages that expanded "Murder Is No Joke" from forty-eight pages to seventy-nine. In "Murder Is No Joke," after murder was committed it was not worth anyone's bother to bring Flora on the scene when Archie visited the offices of Gallant, Inc., to interview the chief suspects. In "Frame-up for Murder" Flora is prominently visible, and her presence makes Archie's day. At the close of this interlude, moreover, Archie struts into Alec Gallant's office and speaks his mind with a bravado remarkable even for Archie. One has to assume that his recent smooching with Flora has produced such a rush of adrenaline that he is ready to take on the world. Perhaps that also accounts for his boast to Emmy Thorne that he can chin himself twenty times.

Nero Wolfe likewise appears to better advantage in the rewrite of "Murder Is No Joke," and not solely because a younger, demure Flora declines to speculate in jaded tones on his sex life. A vital Flora generates more excitement all around. Archie cares more about the case that evolves out of her visit to the brownstone, and so, inevitably, does Wolfe. Wolfe's speculations concerning the authenticity of the phone call made to Bianca Voss come forth more promptly and do not seem, as in "Murder Is No Joke," arrived at through the instigation of Inspector Cramer. The lively exchange of comments between Wolfe and Archie when Bianca's visit ends is also one of the high moments of the rewrite since it has no counterpart in "Murder Is No Joke." One detects, too, that, once drawn into the case, Wolfe becomes, on learning of Alec Gallant's resistance activities in World War II, allied to him in sympathies. Certainly Rex's own commitments in the war years assured both his allegiance to Gallant's principles and his tacit approval of Gallant's initiative taken when the niceties of the law raised the possibility that heinous crimes against humanity would go unpunished.

At one point in "Murder Is No Joke," Nero Wolfe is grossly insulted. He is told, " 'You are scum, I know, in your stinking sewer! Your slimy little ego in your big gob of fat!' " Even Cramer is nonplussed when these phrases are repeated to him. It is easier to believe that the drab and hostile Flora scripted these lines in "Murder Is No Joke" than to attribute them to the vivacious Flora of "Frame-up for Murder." But happily they survived the rewrite, and that kept in the marvelous scene in which Wolfe shows how the word "gob" made him aware that "the extraordinary billingsgate . . . spat at me" was a prepared text. To know the words were spoken only for calculated effect makes everyone feel better—Wolfe as well as the reader. And, really, we could not spare that moment when, after Wolfe's explanation is forthcoming and he gestures at the conclusion, Archie complacently observes, "He waved 'gob' away."

In "Frame-up for Murder," Inspector Cramer is given more to do than he was given in "Murder Is No Joke." We may commend him, perhaps, for his restraint in not pointing out that this attempt to deceive Wolfe repeats an episode from *The Rubber Band*. Perhaps it was Cramer's prudence on this occasion that induced Rex Stout to allow him to speak the words "Murder is no joke," which gave the story its title and accounts, as well, for Wolfe's generous reiteration of these words at a crucial moment in the story. It is surprising to observe, in scrutinizing the original manuscript, that Rex Stout once marked these words for excision. It is more surprising yet, to discover from his notes that originally he had settled on a different murderer. No harm can come from mentioning the name now, because no reasonable reader will see him as a possible suspect. We are referring to Carl Drew! It was a good day's work when Rex changed his mind.

While odd circumstances attended the writing of "Bitter End" and "Frame-up for Murder," the history of one other Wolfe novella is even more unusual—that is, the story serialized as "The Counterfeiter's Knife" in *The Saturday Evening Post*, in the issues for January 14, 21, and 28, 1961. Unaltered, the same story was published the following year as "Counterfeit for Murder" in *Homicide Trinity*, one of the tripartite Wolfe volumes. Rex's Writing Record for this story reads: "73 pp. Began 3/6/59, finished 3/31/59. 9 days out, 17 days writing time." His breakdown of days shows that he actually worked on it on twenty-three different days, but sometimes only for short intervals, which he recorded as fractions of days. Only on the nineteenth and twentieth, when he was in New York, and on the twenty-ninth, Easter Sunday, was he away from his desk entirely. For Rex to give so much time to a single novella was unusual. But we do not have to look far for an explanation. As he noted in his writing record, underlining the word twice for emphasis, the story he wrote in that twenty-six-day interval was a "Rewrite." Just ahead of the entry given above he had recorded these particulars concerning the original version of the story: " 'Counterfeit for Murder'—74 pp. Began 1/22/59, finished 2/11/59. 3 days out, 18 days writing time." Only on two days did he do no writing at all, the twenty-ninth and thirtieth of January, when he had to be in Providence. Fractions of days show that he could have reduced the total of working days by another three, making, in all, five days out. But, all things considered, the work had gone well; so that, quite up to his usual average, he had written four or five pages on twelve of the nineteen days he had written. Nothing in his notes suggests that he was dissatisfied with the results. Yet, less than a month later, he discarded all but the first seven pages of this story and, starting again at that point, took events in a direction so contrary to that in which they had moved before, that the lady who quickened Archie's heartbeat in the original is here hastily dispatched with a bread knife, and the dowdy boardinghouse keeper, who had promptly fallen prey to a hit-and-run motorist in the first version, here escapes with a grazing, is reanimated, and given liberty to engage Wolfe as well as Archie in some of the liveliest dialogue to be found anywhere in the corpus. She, Anthony Boucher said of Miss Hattie Annis, "is the most entertaining client to visit West Thirty-fifth Street in some time." And indeed she was.

A perusal of the two versions of "Counterfeit for Murder" shows that Hattie Annis's reappearance is so thoroughly desirable that it completely justifies Rex Stout's repudiating his folly in snuffing out a character that was endowed with her remarkable vitality. But was that the actual reason for his decision? We can only conjecture because, on July 11, 1972, when I asked Rex why he had rewritten this story, he said, "There must be a reason, but I have forgotten what it was." We know, at least, that Rex was not acting on the advice of anyone else, either editor or friend, because, in the twenty-three-day interval that elapsed between his completing the original and beginning the rewrite, he had shown the manuscript to no one. He arrived at the decision entirely on his own. Only one possible explanation can be offered. In that interval Rex had spent a fishing holiday, at Paradise Island, Florida, with his friend Nathaniel Selleck (the second of the three Nathaniel Sellecks who were Rex's physicians successively over a forty-five-year period). On the day that Rex returned from Florida, word reached him that Dr. Selleck had dropped dead moments after his departure. On receipt of the news Rex resumed writing at once, perhaps, in the creative act of calling back to life someone who had died, resorting to a form of therapy mysterious to some but not at all mysterious to those who write.

Hattie Annis is the most successful of several characters Rex based on his mother's sister, Alice Todhunter Bradley, who as a young woman, in the 1880s, traveled through the West alone, lecturing, serving as schoolmistress to Brigham Young's kin and, eventually, as a confidante to Eugene Debs. In the original "Counterfeit for Murder" Hattie does not meet Nero Wolfe. In the rewrite she not only meets him, she flabbergasts him by asking him for "lamb kidneys *bourguignonne*" when he invites her to lunch. This scene alone justifies the rewrite. Rarely is Nero Wolfe ever put out of countenance by anyone. By story's end Wolfe is won over by Hattie's homely candor and integrity. No mistake about it, Hattie is a straight-arrow.

If it is incumbent on us to ask what else readers gain in the rewrite of "Counterfeit for Murder," the question can at least be speedily answered. Wolfe is given more to do here. Once again he is able to utilize, to good advantage, the services of Saul, Fred, and Orrie, and to stage one of his revealing assemblies. We also learn the source of the counterfeit bills, a detail skimped on in the original story. And, finally, Wolfe is able to compromise severely the dignity of Albert Leach (that his surname recalls a parasite is not accidental), a T-man whose patronizing attitude has awakened his indignation. This scene foreshadows Wolfe's brilliant coup in humbling J. Edgar Hoover, six years later, in *The Doorbell Rang*.

We need not suppose that the rewrite of "Counterfeit for Murder" cannibalized the original, stripping from it its most meritorious parts. Tamaris Baxter, who changes roles with Hattie in the rewrite, to become the needed corpse, is intelligent and resourceful but a bit starchy, probably because she is not the person she pretends to be. To dispense with her is no hardship. But the original story has several wonderful scenes that can ill be spared. The restoration of them to a place in the corpus is a gain that all discriminating Neronians will applaud. Early in the story tensions run high between Wolfe and Archie. Archie comes upon Wolfe studying a terrestrial globe, "probably picking out a place for me to be exiled in." Wolfe fires Archie, and Archie reports, "I turned and marched out, chin up, with my ego patting me on the back, and mounted the stairs to my room." It is a joy to see Wolfe later weasel out of this commitment when he realizes he needs Archie after all.

Midway in the story we are treated to two superb scenes, one treading close on the heels of the other. Albert Leach, accompanied by a team of four other T-men, invades the brownstone and conducts an inch-by-inch search, even to sifting through the files in Wolfe's office and the osmundine in his plant rooms. " 'My house has been invaded, my privacy has been outraged, and my belongings have been pawed,' " Wolfe declares. He locks himself in his bedroom and refuses to emerge until the T-men are gone. Unfortunately, for himself, Inspector Cramer chooses this disagreeable hour—it is eleven thirty at night—to call, and Wolfe, with unprecedented vigor, uses his physical bulk to block his entrance, in what surely is one of the great moments of the saga.

Archie's witty sallies and disclosures, as usual, are sprinkled through the story and add to its zest. It is intriguing to learn that he once spent nine rainy hours in a doorway on a stakeout. At one point he tells us, too,

"I no longer had any illusions about dimples. The most attractive and best-placed ones I had ever seen were on the cheeks of a woman who had fed arsenic to three husbands in a row." The invasion of the brownstone by the T-men sparks some of his most audacious quips. He asks one of them, " 'Did you find the snow in the secret drawer?' " And he also asks the man to turn his mattress because it's due for a turning. He explains further that FBI stands for "Foiled By Intelligence." We cannot pass from the subject of Archie without noting one curious detail attaching to the original manuscript. Archie's crucial maneuver of leaving his hat and coat in Hattie's parlor was, for Rex, an afterthought. He actually taped that detail over the passage it replaced. For Rex such backtracking in his manuscripts was unprecedented.

William S. Baring-Gould surmised that the events recounted in "Counterfeit for Murder" occurred on a Monday and Tuesday in the winter of 1960–1961. He was wrong. Rex's notes show that they occurred in 1959, on Monday, January 26, and Tuesday, January 27. These dates, used in the original, were retained in the rewrite.

The year in which Rex wrote his two versions of "Counterfeit for Murder" was, for him, an annus mirabilis. He wrote three stories in 1958 and three again in 1960. In 1959 he worked on five. "Eeny Meeny Murder Mo," was finished in January. Between January and March he produced his two versions of "Counterfeit for Murder." *Plot It Yourself* was begun in May and finished in July. "The Rodeo Murder" was begun in September and finished in October. A suggestion that he wrote "Counterfeit for Murder" twice because he was unsure of himself can have no validity. Rex was far from being written out. Indeed, he would write another seventeen Nero Wolfe stories, eleven of them novels, before he racked up his quill at eighty-nine. That he could do a second version of "Counterfeit for Murder" and come within ten lines of making it exactly the same length as its predecessor bespeaks a virtuosity that confirms that his mastery over his material was unimpaired.

While Rex was writing "Counterfeit for Murder," his grandsons, Chris and Reed Maroc, aged three and five, were living at High Meadow. When their mother, Rex's daughter Barbara, told them not to bother their grandfather because he was "busy with a counterfeiting plot," they took this literally and invaded Rex's study to confront him with drawn, toy pistols. "They had a point," Rex conceded. "It could be argued that all fiction writing is counterfeiting." When "The Counterfeiter's Knife" was published in *The Saturday Evening Post*, the boys, clad in, respectively, Superman outfit and western gear, restaged their stickup for a photograph to accompany the story. This, Rex explained, did not make them liable to charges of false arrest. "A reconstruction," he said, "is no good as evidence." As encountered in this volume, Rex's own reconstructions, however, are excellent evidence of the fecundity of his genius.

John J. McAleer
Mount Independence
March 25, 1985

BITTER END

In the old brownstone house which was the dwelling, and also contained the office, of Nero Wolfe on West 35th Street near the Hudson River, in New York, heavy gloom had penetrated into every corner of every room, so that there was no escaping from it.

Fritz Brenner was in bed with the grippe.

If it had been Theodore Horstmann, who nursed the 3,000 orchids on the top floor, it would have been merely an inconvenience. If it had been me, Archie Goodwin, secretary, bodyguard, goad, and goat, Wolfe would have been no worse than peevish. But Fritz was the cook; and such a cook that Marko Vukcic of Rusterman's famous restaurant, had once offered a fantastic sum for his release to the major leagues, and met with scornful refusal from Wolfe and Fritz both. On that Tuesday in November the kitchen had not seen him for three days, and the resulting situation was not funny. I'll skip the awful details—for instance, the desperate and disastrous struggle that took place Sunday

afternoon between Wolfe and a couple of ducklings—
and go on with the climax.

It was lunchtime Tuesday. Wolfe and I were at the
dining table. I was doing all right with a can of beans I
had got at the delicatessen. Wolfe, his broad face dour
and dismal, took a spoonful of stuff from a little glass jar
that had just been opened, dabbed it onto the end of a
roll, bit it off, and chewed. All of a sudden, with nothing to warn me, there was an explosion like the burst-
ing of a ten-inch shell. Instinctively I dropped my
sandwich and put up my hands to protect my face, but
too late. Little gobs of the stuff, and particles of masti-
cated roll, peppered me like shrapnel.

I glared at him. "Well," I said witheringly. I removed something from my eyelid with the corner of my
napkin. "If you think for one moment you can get
away—"

I left it hanging. With as black a fury on his face as
any I had ever seen there, he was on his feet and
heading for the kitchen. I stayed in my chair. After I
had done what I could with the napkin, hearing meanwhile the garglings and splashings of Wolfe at the kitchen
sink, I reached for the jar, took a look at the contents,
and sniffed it. I inspected the label. It was small and to
the point:

TINGLEY'S TIDBITS—Since 1981—The Best
Liver Pâté No. 3

I was sniffing at it again when Wolfe marched in
with a tray containing three bottles of beer, a chunk of
cheese, and a roll of salami. He sat down without a
word and started slicing salami.

"The last man who spat at me," I said casually,
"got three bullets in his heart before he hit the floor."

"Pfui," Wolfe said coldly.

"And at least," I continued, "he really meant it. Whereas you were merely being childish and trying to show what a supersensitive gourmet you are—"

"Shut up. Did you taste it?"

"No."

"Do so. It's full of poison."

I regarded him suspiciously. It was ten to one he was stringing me, but, after all, there were a good many people who would have regarded the death of Nero Wolfe as a ray of sunshine in a dark world, and a few of them had made efforts to bring it about. I picked up the jar and a spoon, procured a morsel about the size of a pea, and put it in my mouth. A moment later I discreetly but hastily ejected it into my napkin, went to the kitchen and did some rinsing, returned to the dining-room and took a good large bite from a dill pickle. After the pickle's pungency had to some extent quieted the turmoil in my taste buds, I reached for the jar and smelled it again.

"That's funny," I said

Wolfe made a growling noise.

"I mean," I continued hastily, "that I don't understand it. How could it be some fiend trying to poison you? I bought it at Bruegel's and brought it home myself, and I opened it, and I'd swear the lid hadn't been tampered with. But I don't blame you for spitting, even though I happened to be in the line of fire. If that's Tingley's idea of a rare, exotic flavor to tempt the jaded appetite—"

"That will do, Archie." Wolfe put down his empty glass. I had never heard his tone more menacing. "I am not impressed by your failure to understand this abominable outrage. I might bring myself to tolerate it if some frightened or vindictive person shot me to death, but this is insupportable." He made the growling noise again. "My food. You know my attitude toward food." He aimed a rigid finger at the jar, and his voice trembled with ferocity. "Whoever put that in there is going to regret it."

He said no more, and I concentrated on the beans and pickles and milk. When he had finished the cheese he got up and left the room, taking the third bottle of beer along, and when I was through I cleared the table and went to the kitchen and washed up. Then I proceeded to the office. He had his mass deposited in the oversized chair behind his desk, and was leaning back with his eyes closed and a twist to his lips which showed that the beer descending his gullet had washed no wrath down with it. Without opening his eyes he muttered at me, "Where's that jar?"

"Right here." I put it on his desk.

"Get Mr. Whipple, at the laboratory."

I sat at my desk, and looked up the number and dialed it. When I told Wolfe I had Whipple he got himself upright and reached for his phone and spoke to it:

"Mr. Whipple? . . . This is Nero Wolfe. Good afternoon, sir. Can you do an analysis for me right away? . . . I don't know. It's a glass jar containing a substance which I foolishly presumed to be edible. . . . I have no idea. Mr. Goodwin will take it down to you immediately."

I was glad to have an errand that would take me away from that den of dejection for an hour or so, but something more immediate intervened. The doorbell rang and, since Fritz was out of commission, I went to answer it. Swinging the front door open, I found myself confronted by something pleasant. While she didn't reach the spectacular and I'm not saying that I caught

4

my breath, one comprehensive glance at her gave me the feeling that it was foolish to regard the world as an abode of affliction merely because Fritz had the grippe. Her cheeks had soft in-curves and her eyes were a kind of chartreuse, something the color of my bathroom walls upstairs. They looked worried.

"Hello," I said enthusiastically.

"Mr. Nero Wolfe?" she asked in a nice voice from west of Pittsburgh. "My name is Amy Duncan."

I knew it was hopeless. With Wolfe in a state of mingled rage and despondency, and with the bank balance in a flourishing condition, if I had gone and told him that a good-looking girl named Duncan wanted to see him, no matter what about, he would only have been churlish. Whereas there was a chance . . . I invited her in, escorted her down the hall and into the office, and pulled up a chair for her.

"Miss Duncan, Mr. Wolfe," I said, and sat down. "She wants to ask you something."

Wolfe, not even glancing at her, glared at me. "Confound you!" he muttered. "I'm engaged. I'm busy." He transferred it to the visitor: "Miss Duncan, you are the victim of my assistant's crack-brained impudence. So am I. I see people only by appointment."

She smiled at him. "I'm sorry, but now that I'm here it won't take long—"

"No." His eyes came back to me. "Archie, when you have shown Miss Duncan out, come back here."

He was obviously completely out of control. As for that, I was somewhat edgy myself, after the three days I had just gone through and it looked to me as if a little cooling off might be advisable before any further interchange of sentiments. So I arose and told him firmly, "I'll run along down to the laboratory. Maybe I can give Miss Duncan a lift." I picked up the jar. "Do you want me to wait—?"

*   *   *

"Where did you get that?" Amy Duncan said.

I looked at her in astonishment. "Get it? This jar?"

"Yes. Where did you get it?"

"Bought it. Sixty-five cents."

"And you're taking it to a laboratory? Why? Does it taste funny? Oh, I'll bet it does! Bitter?"

I gawked at her in amazement. Wolfe, upright, his eyes narrowed at her, snapped, "Why do you ask that?"

"Because," she said, "I recognized the label. And taking it to a laboratory—that's what I came to see you about! Isn't that odd? A jar of it right here—"

On any other man Wolfe's expression would have indicated a state of speechlessness, but I have never yet seen him flabbergasted to a point where he was unable to articulate. "Do you mean to say," he demanded, "that you were actually aware of this infamous plot? That you knew of this unspeakable insult to my palate and my digestion?"

"Oh, no! But I know it has quinine in it."

"Quinine!" he roared.

She nodded. "I suppose so." She stretched a hand toward me. "May I look at it?" I handed her the jar. She removed the lid, took a tiny dab of the contents on the tip of her little finger, licked it off with her tongue, and waited for the effect. It didn't take long. "Br-r-uh!" she said, and swallowed twice. "It sure is bitter. That's it, all right." She put the jar on the desk. "How very odd—"

"Not odd," Wolfe said grimly. "*Odd* is not the word. You say it has quinine in it. You knew that as soon as you saw it. Who put it in?"

"I don't know. That's what I came to see you for, to ask you to find out. You see, it's my uncle— May I tell you about it?"

6

"You may."

She started to wriggle out of her coat, and I helped her with it and got it out of her way so she could settle back in her chair. She thanked me with a friendly little smile containing no trace of quinine, and I returned to my desk and got out a notebook and flipped to a blank page.

"Arthur Tingley," she said, "is my uncle. My mother's brother. He owns Tingley's Tidbits. And he's such a pigheaded—" She flushed. "Well, he is pigheaded. He actually suspects me of having something to do with that quinine, just because—for no reason at all!"

"Are you saying," Wolfe demanded incredulously, "that the scoundrel, knowing that his confounded tidbits contain quinine, continues to distribute them?"

"No," she shook her head, "he's not a scoundrel. That's not it. It was only a few weeks ago that they learned about the quinine. Complaints began to come in, and thousands of jars were returned from all over the country. He had them analyzed, and lots of them contained quinine. Of course, it was only a small proportion of the whole output—it's a pretty big business. He tried to investigate it, and Miss Yates—she's in charge of production—took all possible precautions, but it's happened again in recent shipments."

"Where's the factory?"

"Not far from here. On West Twenty-sixth Street near the river."

"Do you work there?"

"No, I did once, when I first came to New York, but I—I quit."

"Do you know what the investigation has disclosed?"

"Nothing. Not really. My uncle suspects—I guess he suspects everybody, even his son Philip, his adopted son. And me! It's simply ridiculous! But chiefly he

7

suspects a man—a vice-president of P. & B., the Provisions & Beverages Corporation. Tingley's Tidbits is an old-established business—my great-grandfather founded it seventy years ago—and P. & B. has been trying to buy it, but my uncle wouldn't sell. He thinks they bribed someone in the factory to put in the quinine to scare him into letting go. He thinks that Mr.—the vice-president I spoke of—did it."

"Mr.—?"

"Mr. Cliff. Leonard Cliff."

I glanced up from my notebook on account of a slight change in the key of her voice.

Wolfe inquired, "Do you know Mr. Cliff?"

"Oh, yes." She shifted in her chair. "That is, I—I'm his secretary."

"Indeed." Wolfe's eyes went shut and then opened again halfway. "When you left your uncle's employ you came to terms with the enemy?"

She flared up. "Of course not!" she said indignantly. "You sound like my uncle! I had to have a job, didn't I? I was born and brought up in Nebraska. Three years ago my mother died, and I came to New York and started to work in my uncle's office. I stuck it out for two years, but it got—unpleasant, and either I quit or he fired me, it would be hard to say which. I got a job as a stenographer with P. & B., and six weeks ago I was promoted and I'm now Mr. Cliff's secretary. If you want to know why it got so unpleasant in my uncle's office—"

"I don't. Unless it has a bearing on this quinine business."

"It hasn't. None whatever."

"But you are sufficiently concerned about the quinine to come to me about it. Why?"

"Because my uncle is such a—" She stopped, biting her lip. "You don't know him. He writes to my

8

father, things about me that aren't so, and my father writes and threatens to come to New York—it's such a mess! I certainly didn't put quinine in his darned Tidbits! I suppose I'm prejudiced, but I don't believe any investigating he does will ever get anywhere, and the only way to stop it is for someone to investigate who knows how." She flashed a smile at him. "Which brings me to the embarrassing part of it. I haven't got much money—"

"You have something better," Wolfe grunted.

"Better?"

"Yes. Luck. The thing you want to know is the thing I had determined to find out before I knew you existed. I had already told Mr. Goodwin that the blackguard who poisoned that pâté is going to regret it." He grimaced. "I can still taste it. Can you go now with Mr. Goodwin to your uncle's factory and introduce him?"

"I—" She glanced at her watch and hesitated. "I'll be awfully late getting back to the office. I only asked for an hour—"

"Very well. Archie, show Miss Duncan out and return for instructions." . . .

It was barely three o'clock when I reached the base of operations, and the jar in my pocket was only half full, for I had first gone downtown to the laboratory and left a sample for analysis.

The three-story brick building on West 26th Street was old and grimy-looking, with a cobbled driveway for trucks tunneled through its middle. Next to the driveway were three stone steps leading up to a door with an inscription in cracked and faded paint:

TINGLEY'S TIDBITS OFFICE

As I parked the roadster and got out, I cocked an admiring eye at a Crosby town car, battleship gray, with license GJ88, standing at the curb. "Comes the revolution," I thought, "I'll take that first." I had my foot on the first stone step leading up to the office when the door opened and a man emerged. I had the way blocked. At a glance, it was hard to imagine anyone calling him Uncle Arthur, with his hard, clamped jaw and his thin, hard mouth, but, not wanting to miss my quarry, I held the path and addressed him: "Mr. Arthur Tingley?"

"No," he said in a totalitarian tone, shooting a haughty glance at me as he brushed by, with cold, keen eyes of the same battleship gray as his car. I remembered, just in time, that I had in my pocket a piece of yellow chalk which I had been marking orchid pots with that morning. Circling around him, I beat him to the car door which the liveried chauffeur was holding open and with two swift swipes chalked a big X on the elegant enamel.

"Don't monkey with that," I said sternly, and, before either of them could produce words or actions, beat it up the stone steps and entered the building.

It sure was a ramshackle joint. From a dingy hall a dilapidated stair went up. I mounted to the floor above, heard noises, including machinery humming, off somewhere, and through a rickety door penetrated a partition and was in an anteroom. From behind a grilled window somebody's grandpa peered out at me, and by shouting I managed to convey to him that I wanted to see Mr. Arthur Tingley. After a wait I was told that Mr. Tingley was busy, and would be indefinitely. On a leaf of my notebook I wrote, "Quinine urgent," and sent it in. That did it. After another wait a cross-eyed young man came and guided me through a labyrinth of partitions and down a hall into a room.

Seated at an old, battered roll-top desk was a man talking into a phone, and in a chair facing him was a woman older than him with the physique and facial equipment of a top sergeant. Since the phone conversation was none of my business, I stood and listened to it, and gathered that someone named Philip had better put in an appearance by five o'clock or else. Meanwhile I surveyed the room, which had apparently been thrown in by the Indians when they sold the island. By the door, partly concealed by a screen, was an old, veteran marble-topped washstand. A massive, old-fashioned safe was against the wall across from Tingley's desk. Wooden cupboards, and shelves loaded down with the accumulation of centuries, occupied most of the remaining wall space.

"Who the hell are you?"

I whirled and advanced. "A man by the name of Goodwin. Archie. The question is, do you want the *Gazette* to run a feature article about quinine in Tidbits, or do you want to discuss it first?"

His mouth fell open. "The *Gazette*?"

"Right. Circulation over a million."

"Good God!" he said in a hollow and helpless tone. The woman glared at me.

I was stirred by compassion. He may have merited his niece's opinion of him, expressed and implied, but he was certainly a pathetic object at that moment.

I sat down. "Be of good cheer," I said encouragingly. "The *Gazette* hasn't got it yet. That's merely one of the possibilities I offer in case you start shoving. I represent Nero Wolfe."

"Nero Wolfe, the detective?"

"Yes. He started to eat—"

* * *

The woman snorted. "I've been expecting this. Didn't I warn you, Arthur? Blackmail." She squared her jaw at me. "Who are you working for? P. & B.? Consolidated Cereals?"

"Neither one. Are you Miss Yates?"

"I am. And you can take—"

"Pardon me." I grinned at her. "Pleased to meet you. I'm working for Nero Wolfe. He took a mouthful of Liver Pâté Number Three, with painful consequences. He's very fussy about his food. He wants to speak to the person who put in the quinine."

"So do I," Tingley said grimly.

"You don't know. Do you?"

"No."

"But you'd like to know?"

"You're damn' right I would."

"Okay. I come bearing gifts. If you hired Wolfe for this job, granting he'd take it, it would cost you a fortune. But he's vindictive. He wishes to do things to this quinine jobber. I was sent here to look around and ask questions."

Tingley wearily shook his head. He looked at Miss Yates. She looked at him. "Do you believe him?" Tingley asked her.

"No," she declared curtly. "Is it likely—?"

"Of course not," I cut her off. "Nothing about Nero Wolfe is likely, which is why I tolerate him. It's not likely, but that's how it is. You folks are comical. You're having the services of the best detective in the country offered to you gratis, and listen to you. I'm telling you, Wolfe's going to get this quinine peddler. With your co-operation, fine. Without it, we'll have to start by opening things up with a little publicity, which is why I mentioned the *Gazette*."

Tingley groaned. Miss Yates's shrewd eyes met mine. "What questions do you want to ask?"

"All I can think of. Preferably starting with you two."

"I'm busy. I ought to be out in the factory right now. Did you say you had an appointment, Arthur?"

"Yes." Tingley shoved back his chair and got up. "I have—I have to go somewhere." He got his hat from a hook on the wall beside his desk, and his coat from another one. "I'll be back by four-thirty." He struggled into his coat and confronted me. His hat was on crooked. "If Miss Yates wants to talk to you, she can tell you as much as I could. I'm about half out of my senses. If this is an infernal trick of that P. & B. outfit—" He darted to his desk, turned a key in a bottom drawer, pocketed the key, and made for the door. On the threshold he turned: "You handle it, Gwen."

So her name was Gwendolyn, or maybe Guinevere. It certainly must have been given to her when she was quite young—say sixty years ago. She was imperturbably and efficiently collecting an asortment of papers Tingley had left scattered on his desk and anchoring them under a cylindrical chunk of metal with a figure 2 on it, a weight from an old-fashioned balance scale. She straightened and met my gaze:

"I've been after him to get a detective, and he wouldn't do it. This thing has got to be stopped. It's awful. I've been here all my life—been in charge of the factory for twenty years—and now—" She squared her jaw. "Come along."

I followed her. We left by another door than the one I had entered by, traversed a hall, passed through a door at the end, and there we were, in the Tidbits maternity ward. Two hundred women and girls, maybe more, in white smocks, were working at tables and benches and various kinds of vats and machines. Miss Yates led me down an aisle and she stopped beside a large vat. A woman about my age who had been peering into the vat turned to face us.

"This is Miss Murphy, my assistant," Miss Yates said brusquely. "Carrie, this is Mr. Goodwin, a detective. Answer any questions he wants to ask, except about our formulas, and show him anything he wants to see." She turned to me. "I'll talk with you later, after I get some mixes through."

I caught a flicker of something, hesitation or maybe apprehension, in Miss Murphy's eyes, but it went as fast as it came, and she said quietly, "Very well, Miss Yates." . . .

Wolfe was sticking to his accustomed daily schedule, in a sort of stubborn desperation in spite of the catastrophe of Fritz's grippe. Mornings from 9 to 11 and afternoons from 4 to 6 he spent up in the plant rooms. When he came down at six that afternoon I was in the office waiting for him.

He stopped in the middle of the room, glanced around, frowned at me, and said, "Dr. Vollmer states that Fritz can get up in the morning. Not today. Not for dinner. Where is Mr. Tingley?"

"I don't know."

"I told you to bring him here."

He was using his most provocative tone. I could have put quinine in his food. I said, "It's a good thing Fritz will be up tomorrow. This couldn't go on much longer. Tingley is on the verge of a nervous breakdown. He went out soon after I got there. Miss Yates, whose name is Gwendolyn, the factory superintendent, and her assistant, Miss Carrie Murphy, showed me around. I have just finished typing a detailed report, but there's nothing in it but facts. Tingley returned about four-thirty, but when I tried to see him he was having a talk with his son and I was thrown out on my ear. I'm going back in the morning if I'm still working for you. Those in favor of my resigning, raise their hand." I stuck my hand up high.

"Pfui!" Wolfe said. "A man sells poisoned food—"

"Quinine is not poison."

"A man sells poisoned food and you leave him sitting comfortably in conversation with his son. Now I'm going to the kitchen and try to prepare something to eat. If you care to join—"

"No, thanks. I've got a date. Don't wait up for me."

I went to the hall and got my hat and coat and beat it. From the garage on Tenth Avenue I took the sedan instead of the roadster, drove to Pietro's on 39th Street, and operated on a dish of spaghetti and half a bushel of salad. That made me feel better. When I reached the sidewalk again it was raining, with cold November gusts whipping it around, so I skedaddled around the corner into a newsreel theater. But I was not at peace. There had been enough justification for Wolfe's crack—say one percent—to make it rankle.

My watch said a quarter to eight. I went to the lobby and got out my memo book and turned to the page where, following habit, I had entered the names and addresses of persons connected with the current proceeding. Tingley lived at 691 Sullivan Street. There was no point in phoning, since the idea was to get him and deliver him. I went to the sedan and headed downtown in the rain.

It was an old brick house, painted blue, probably the residence of his father and grandfather before him. A colored maid told me that he wasn't home, hadn't shown up for dinner, and might be at his office. It began to look like no soap, but it was only a little out of the way, so when I got to 26th Street I turned west. Rolling to the curb directly in front of the Tingley

Building, it looked promising; lights showed at a couple of the upstairs windows. I dived through the rain across the sidewalk, found the door unlocked, and entered.

A light was on there in the hall, and I started for the stairs. But with my foot on the first step I stopped; for I had glanced up, and saw something so unexpected that I goggled like a fish. Standing there halfway up, facing me, was Amy Duncan. Her face was white, her eyes were glassy, and she was clinging to the rail with both hands and swaying from side to side.

"Hold it!" I said sharply, and started up. Before I could reach her she lost it. Down she came, rolling right into me. I gathered her up and went back down and stretched her out on the floor. She was out cold, but when I felt her pulse it was pretty good. Routine faint, I thought, and then took it back when I saw a large lump on the side of her head above her right ear.

That made it different. I straightened up. She had unquestionably been conked.

I ascended the steps one at a time, looking for the birdie. There was a light in the upper hall also in the anteroom. I called out, and got no reply. The door leading within was standing open, and I marched through and kept going through more open doors and down the inside hall to the entrance to Tingley's office. That door too stood open and the room was lit, but from the threshold no one was in sight. It occurred to me that the screen, at right angles to the wall, would do nicely for an ambush, so I etered sideways, facing it, and circled around the end of it for a survey just in case.

A mouse ran up my backbone. Tingley was there on the floor alongside the screen, his head toward the marble washstand, and if the head was still connected with the body it must have been at the back, which I couldn't see. There was certainly no connection left in front.

I took a couple of breaths and swallowed saliva, as a sort of priming for my internal processes, which had momentarily stopped.

The blood from the gash in his throat had spread over the floor, running in red tongues along the depressions in the old warped boards, and I stepped wide of it to get around to the other end of him. Squatting beside him for an inspection, I ascertained two facts: He had a lump at the back of his skull and the skin had been broken there, and he was good and dead. I straightened up and collected a few more items with my eyes:

1. A bloody towel on the floor by the washstand, sixteen inches from the wall.

2. Another bloody towel on the rim of the basin, to the right.

3. A knife with a long, thin blade and a black composition handle on the floor between the body and the screen. In the factory that afternoon I had seen girls slicing meat loaves with knives like it.

4. On the floor between the two front legs of the washstand, a cylinder of metal with a "2" on it. It was Tingley's paperweight.

5. Farther away, out beyond the edge of the screen, a woman's snakeskin handbag. I had seen that before, too, when Amy Duncan called at Wolfe's office.

Circling around the mess again, I picked up the handbag and stuffed it in my pocket, and took a look at the rest of the room. I didn't touch anything, but someone else had. A drawer of the rolltop desk had been jerked out onto the floor. The door of the enormous old safe was standing wide open. Things on the shelves had been pulled off and scattered. Tingley's felt hat was on the wall hook at the left of his desk, but his overcoat was in a heap on the floor.

I looked at my watch. It was 8:22. I would have liked to do a little more inspecting, but if Amy Duncan should come to and beat it . . .

She hadn't. When I got back downstairs she was still there stretched out. I felt her pulse again, buttoned up her coat, made sure her hat was fastened on, and picked her up. I opened the door and got through without bumping her, navigated the steps, and crossed the sidewalk to the car, and stood there with her in my arms a moment, thinking the rain on her face might revive her. The next thing I knew I damn' near needed reviving myself. Something socked me on the side of the jaw from behind.

I went down, not from compulsion but from choice, to get rid of my burden. When I bobbed up again I left Amy on the sidewalk and leaped aside as a figure hurled itself at me. When I side-stepped he lost balance, but recovered and tore at me again. I feinted with my left and he grabbed for it, and my right took him on the button.

He went down and didn't bounce. I dashed back to the stone steps and closed the door, returned, and opened the rear door of the car and lifted Amy in, and wheeled as he regained his feet, started for me, and yelled for help and police, all at once. He obviously knew as much about physical combat as. I did about pearl diving, so I turned him around and from behind locked his arms with my left one and choked his throat with my right, and barked into his ear, "One more squawk and out go the lights! You have one chance to live. Behave yourself and do what I tell you to." I made sure he had no gun before I loosened the hook on his neck. He didn't vocalize, so I released him. "Open that car door—"

I meant the front door, but before I could stop him he had the rear one open and most of himself inside and was bleating like a goat, "Amy! Good God, she's—Amy—"

I reached in for a shoulder and yanked him out and banged the door and opened the front one. "She's alive," I said, "but you won't be in five seconds. Get in there and fold yourself under the dash. I'm taking her to a doctor and you're going along."

He got in. I pushed him down and forward, disregarding his sputtering, wriggled back of him to the driver's seat, pulled the door to, and started the car. In two minutes we were at 35th Street, and in another two we rolled to the curb in front of Wolfe's house. I let him come up for air.

"The program," I said, "is as follows: I'll carry her, and you precede me up those steps to that door. If you cut and run I'll drop her—"

He glared at me. His spirit was 'way ahead of his flesh. "I'm not going to cut and run—"

"Okay. Me out first."

He helped me get her out and he wanted to carry her, but I shooed him on ahead through the rain and told him to push the button. When the door opened Wolfe, himself, stood there. At sight of the stranger his colossal frame blocked the way, but when he saw me he fell back and made room for us to enter.

The stranger began, "Are you a doc—?"

"Shut up!" I told him. I faced Wolfe, and observed that he was sustaining his reputation for being impervious to startlement. "I suppose you recognize Miss Duncan. She's been hit on the head. If you will please

phone Doc Vollmer? I'll take her up to the south room."
I made for the elevator, and when the stranger tagged
along I let him. In the south room, two flights up, we
got her onto the bed and covered up.

The stranger was still standing by the bed staring
down at her when Doc Vollmer arrived. After feeling
her pulse and glancing under her eyelid, Doc said he
thought it would be a long time till the funeral and we
wouldn't be needed for a while, so I told the stranger to
come on. He left the room with me and kindly permitted me to close the door, but then announced that he
was going to stay right there outside the door until the
doctor had brought her to.

"You," I said, "might as well learn to face facts.
You know damn' well I could throw you downstairs. If I
do you'll have to go to bed, too. March!"

He marched, but he sure hated it. I followed him
down, and into the office. Wolfe was there at his desk,
looking imperturbable, but when he saw us he started
rubbing his chin, which meant he was boiling inside.

"Sit down," I told the stranger. "This is Mr. Nero
Wolfe. What's your name?"

"None of your damned business!" he informed me.
"This is the most outrageous—!"

"You bet it is. When you rushed me from behind,
you must have come from inside the building. Didn't
you?"

"That's none of your business, either!"

"You're wrong, brother. But I'll try again. Why did
you kill Arthur Tingley?"

He gawked at me. "Are you crazy?"

"Not a bit. Stop me if you've heard it before. I
went there to get Tingley and bring him here to see
Mr. Wolfe. Amy Duncan was there on the stairs looking doubtful. She fell and I caught her, and left her on
the hall floor while I went up to investigate. Tingley

was on the floor of his office with his throat cut. After a brief inspection I returned to Amy and carried her out, and was putting her in the car when you attacked me from behind. You must have come from somewhere. Why not from inside the building? The idea appeals to me."

The stranger had decided he could use a chair, and sank into one. "You say—" He swallowed. "Are you telling the truth?"

"Yes, sir."

"Tingley—with his throat cut? Dead?"

"Very dead." I turned to Wolfe: "He pretended to be going on the theory that I was kidnapping Amy. He's all for Amy. I brought him along because I thought you might need him."

Wolfe was glaring at me: "And why should I need him?"

"Well, he was there. He must have come out of that building. He probably murdered Tingley—"

"And what if he did?"

"Oh. So that's how you feel about it."

"It is. I am under no obligation to catch murderers indiscriminately. Phone the police. Tell them Miss Duncan and this gentleman are here and they can—"

"No!" the stranger blurted.

"No?" Wolfe lifted a brow at him. "Why not?"

"Because it's—Good God! And Amy— You can't—"

"Hold it," I commanded him. "I'm doing this." I grinned at Wolfe. "Okay, boss; I'll call the cops. I merely thought you might like to chat with this bird first, since it seemed likely that whoever killed Tingley also put quinine in your food."

"Ah," Wolfe murmured. "That abominable—" He wiggled a finger at the victim. "Did you poison that liver pâté?"

"I did not."

"Who are you? What's your name?"

"Cliff. Leonard Cliff."

"Indeed. You're a vice-president of the Provisions & Beverage Corporation. Mr. Tingley, himself, suspected you of adulterating his product."

"I know he did. He was wrong. So is this man wrong when he says I must have come out of that building. I wasn't inside the building at all."

"Where were you?"

"I was in the driveway. There's a driveway tunnel near the door. I was in there."

"What were you doing there?"

"Keeping out of the rain. Look here," Cliff said appealingly. "I can't think straight. This is terrible! If Tingley has been murdered the police have to be notified, I know that, but for God's sake don't get them here now! With Miss Duncan—Let me get her to a hospital! And get a lawyer—"

Wolfe cut him off: "What were you doing in the driveway?"

He shook his head. "It had no connection—"

"Pfui! Don't be a fool. If you adulterated Mr. Tingley's product, or cut his throat, either or both, I advise you to get out of here at once. If you didn't, I advise you to answer my questions promptly and fully. Not to mention truthfully. Well, sir? . . . Archie, call police headquarters. I'll talk."

I dialed the number, and when I had it, Wolfe took it at his instrument. "Hello. . . . This is Nero Wolfe. Write this down: Arthur Tingley. His office at his place—"

"Wait!" Cliff blurted. "I'll answer your questions—" He started from his chair, but I got in between him and the desk and he subsided.

Wolfe continued: "—his place of business at Twenty-sixth Street and Tenth Avenue. He's there dead. Murdered. . . . Let me finish, please. My assistant, Archie Goodwin, was there and saw him. Mr. Goodwin had to leave, but he will be here at my home later. . . . No. I have no idea."

He pushed the phone away, and regarded Cliff with his eyes half closed. "You had better make it as succinct as possible. What were you doing in the driveway?"

Cliff was on the edge of his chair, straight, rigid, meeting his gaze. "I was waiting for Miss Duncan to come out. I had followed her there."

"Followed? Without her knowledge?"

"Yes."

"Why?"

Cliff's jaw worked. "I had a dinner engagement with her, and she phoned me at six o'clock and broke it. The reason she gave sounded phony, and I was—damn it, I was jealous! I went to where she lives, on Grove Street, and waited across the street. When she came out it had started to rain, and she took a taxi, and I managed to grab one and follow her. She went straight to Tingley's and dismissed her cab and went in. I did the same, but I went in the tunnel entrance and waited there. I couldn't imagine what she was doing there."

"What time did she arrive?"

"A few minutes after seven. It was one minute to seven when she left her place on Grove Street. When I saw a man drive up and go in, and a little later come out carrying her and start to put her in his car, naturally I went for him."

"Naturally," Wolfe said. "Were you in the tunnel while Miss Duncan was inside?"

"Yes. And I saw three men come and go in and leave again. Goodwin was the last one. There were two others before that."

*   *   *

Wolfe shook his head. "I doubt if that's a good idea. If you invent a constant stream of visitors, and it develops—"

"I'm not inventing, damn it! I saw them!"

"Tell me about them."

"The first one was at seven-thirty. A big, gray town car stopped at the curb, and the driver got out and held an umbrella over another man as he crossed the sidewalk to the entrance. In five minutes the man came out again and ran to the car and got in, and the car drove off. The license was GJ88."

I grunted. They looked at me. "Nothing," I said, "go ahead."

"I nearly missed seeing the second one go in, because he was walking. He had on a raincoat. It was seven-forty when he entered, and he was inside seven or eight minutes. When he came out I got a pretty good view of his face by a street light. He walked off to the east."

"Did you recognize either of the men?"

"No. But that license number—"

"Do you know it?"

"No, but I can guess, on account of the GJ. I think it belongs to Guthrie Judd. It can be checked."

"Guthrie Judd, the banker?"

"He calls himself a banker, yes. He's more of a promoter. He's been boosting an outfit he calls Consolidated Cereals. Recently he's been after the Tingley business. He's shrewd and unscrupulous—and tough."

"Was it Judd who entered the building at seven-thirty?"

"I couldn't tell. The driver was holding an umbrella over him."

Wolfe grunted. "That's prudent. Should you claim to have recognized Judd, and he is able to prove—"

"I'm telling the truth!" Cliff got spirited again. "I'm telling you exactly what happened! Do you think I'm a damned idiot?" He stood up. "I'm going upstairs."

A voice behind him asked, "May I come in?"

It was Doc Vollmer. At Wolfe's nod he entered, his bag in his hand, and spoke professionally: "She'll do all right. She got a bad knock on the head, but there's no fracture. It seems to be nervous shock more than anything. After a night's rest—"

"Is she conscious?" Cliff demanded.

"Oh, yes." Cliff was darting off, but the doctor grabbed his arm. "Now, wait a minute—just take it easy—"

"Can she be moved?" Wolfe inquired.

"I wouldn't advise it. Not tonight."

"I want to ask her some questions."

"Now? Is it urgent?"

"Fairly urgent. The police will be here pretty soon."

"I see. All right, I'd better go up with you. You'll have to go easy with her."

We moved. Wolfe headed for the elevator and the rest of us walked up the two flights. We got there first. Amy, lying on her side, opened her eyes at us, with no indication of interest for Doc or me, but when they lit on Cliff they opened wide and she made a noise.

"Amy!" Cliff squawked. "Thank God! Amy—"

Vollmer held him back.

"You—" she said weakly. "Where—you—I don't—"

"Take her hand," Vollmer said judiciously. "Hold her hand. Don't talk."

Wolfe came in, and Amy moved her head enough to get him in view. "Hello, there," she squeaked.

"Good evening, Miss Duncan," he said politely. "Does it hurt much?"

"Not—well—it aches."

"I suppose so. Can you understand words?"

"Yes—but I don't understand—"

"Please listen. You said nothing this afternoon of any intention to go to your uncle's place this evening. But at seven o'clock you went. Why?"

"He phoned—and asked me to come. Soon after I got home from work."

"What for? Did he say?"

"He said it was something about Phil. My cousin." She went to move her head, and a little moan came out of her. "He wouldn't say what it was on the phone."

"But when you got there? What did he say then?"

"He didn't—oh—"

"Take it easy now," Doc Vollmer warned.

"I'm all right," Amy declared. "I'm not going to faint again. But when I shut my eyes I see it. The door of his office was open and the light was on, but he wasn't there. I mean—I didn't see him. I went right on in."

"Go ahead."

"That's all I remember. The next thing I remember was my head. I thought something was on it holding it down. I tried to lift myself up and then I saw him. Oh!" Her brow creased. "I thought I saw him—my uncle—there with the blood—"

"That's all right. Don't worry about that. What happened next?"

"Nothing happened. I don't remember anything."

"Didn't you see anyone at all when you went in? Or hear anyone?"

"No. I don't think—I'm sure I didn't—"

"Excuse me," I said. "The doorbell's ringing. If it's city employees do I ask to see a warrant?"

"No." Wolfe scowled at me. "Take them to the office. . . . Wait a minute. Dr. Vollmer, if this young woman is in no condition to leave my house it would be cruel and dangerous for her to undergo a police grilling. Do you agree?"

"I do."

"Good. . . . Miss Duncan, when a policeman comes up here to look at you, keep your eyes closed and moan. Will you do that?"

"Yes. But—"

"No buts. Don't overdo it, and don't speak." He moved. "Come, gentlemen."

When we got downstairs I waited until they were in the office before opening the front door. There I was greeted by a surprise. It was no squad lieutenant, but Inspector Cramer himself, who shoved in rudely over the sill, with a pair of dicks on his heels. All he had for me was a discourteous remark about answering doorbells as he made for the office. Having to shut the door, I brought up the rear.

Crammer appeared to be having an attack of gout. Not bothering to pass the time of day, he barked at me like a howitzer, "What were you doing down at Twenty-sixth Street?"

I looked at the boss. He murmured, "He's upset, Archie. Humor him."

"Humor hell! What time did you get there?"

I looked thoughtful. "Well, let's see . . ."

"Quit clowning! You know damn well you've always got a timetable!"

"Yes, sir," I said abjectly. "Arrived at 8:08. Left at 8:24."

"You admit it!"

"Admit it? I'm proud of it. It was quick work."

"Yeah." If glares could kill, I would have been awful sick. "And Wolfe phoned from here at five after nine! You didn't see the phone right there on Tingley's desk? I've warned you about that. Now, talk! Fast!"

Having received no flag from Wolfe to retain any

DEATH TIMES THREE

items for our personal use, I gave Cramer the crop, as far as my activities and observations were concerned, omitting the crumbs that had been gathered in conversation with Cliff and Amy. My candor didn't seem to make him any more friendly.

When I finished he grunted vulgarly. "So you stood there in that room with a man lying there murdered; and a phone right there and you didn't use it. . . . Where's the woman?"

"Upstairs in bed."

"You can check her out. Doyle, stay here with Mr. Cliff. Foster, come with me—well?"

Doc Vollmer blocked the way. He said firmly, "Miss Duncan should not be disturbed. I speak as her physician."

"You do." Cramer eyed him. "I'll take a look at her. Come, Foster."

Doc Vollmer, leading the way, went with the forces of law and order. Wolfe heaved a sigh, leaned back, and closed his eyes. Pretty soon steps were heard descending the stairs, and Cramer and Vollmer entered. Wolfe opened his eyes.

"She's faking," Cramer declared. "Sure as hell. I'll send a police doctor."

"Dr. Vollmer," Wolfe murmured, "is a competent and reputable physician."

"Yeah, I know. And a friend of yours. I'll send a police doctor. And I'm taking Goodwin and Cliff downtown."

"Where's that man you had with you?"

"Upstairs. On a chair outside Miss Duncan's door. He's going to stay there. And no one but the doctor is going either in or out."

Wolfe's bulk became upright. "This is my house, Mr. Cramer," he said icily, "and you can't use it for the persecution of innocent and battered females. That man can't stay here."

"Try and put him out," Cramer said grimly. "Next time Goodwin stumbles on a man with his head cut off, maybe he'll let us know the same day. . . . Come on, you two." . . .

At ten o'clock the following morning we didn't have a guest any more, but we had a client. Having been kept at headquarters until three A.M., I was peevish from lack of sleep. Fritz was on his feet again, but unstable from his grippe. Wolfe was a seething volcano from a sense of outrage. He had had the minor satisfaction of refusing admission to the police doctor the night before, but at eight in the morning they had come with a warrant for Amy Duncan as a material witness and carted her off, and all he could do was grind his teeth. So when I told him, as he sat propped up in bed sipping chocolate and glowering like a thunderhead, that down at headquarters Leonard Cliff had hired him, through me, to go to work, he didn't even blink an eye. His method of starting the job was customary and characteristic:

"Have Mr. Guthrie Judd here at eleven."

Before leaving the office I typed what seemed to me to be a nifty visiting card:

Mr. Judd: I respectfully submit the following schedule of events last evening at the Tingley Building:

7:05: Amy Duncan arrives; is knocked on head.
7:30: Guthrie Judd arrives.
7:35: Guthrie Judd leaves.
8:08: I arrive, find Tingley dead.
　　　　　　　　May I discuss it with you?
　　　　　　　　　　　Archie Goodwin.

I phoned his office in the financial district a little after nine, but was unable to extract any information from anyone even about the weather, which was fine, so I got out the roadster and drove down there.

After a supercilious receptionist condescended to phone someone, and a sap with slick hair made sure I wasn't Jesse James, I got the envelope dispatched. Then I waited, until finally a retired prize fighter appeared and conducted me through doors and down corridors, and ushered me into a room about the size of a tennis court; and he stayed right at my elbow for the trip across a couple of acres of rugs to where a man sat at an enormous flat-topped desk with nothing on it but a newspaper. On the man's face was the same totalitarian expression that had goaded me into chalking an X on the door of his car the day before. The corner of the card I had typed was held between the tips of a finger and thumb to avoid germs.

"This impertinence," he said, in a tone he must have been practicing from boyhood, in case he had ever been a boy. "I wanted to look at you. Take him out, Aiken."

I grinned at him. "I forgot to bring my chalk. But you're already down. You'll discuss it either with me or the police—"

"Bah. The police have already informed me of Mr. Cliff's false and ridiculous statement. Also, they have just told me on the phone who you are. If you annoy me further I'll have you jailed. Take him out, Aiken."

The ex-pug actually put his hand on my arm. It was all I could do to keep from measuring one of the rugs with him. But I merely set my jaw and walked back across the carpet department to the door. He accompanied me all the way to the elevators. As the elevator door opened I said in a kindly tone, "Here, boy," and flipped a nickel at his face. It got him on the tip of the nose, but luckily his reflex was too slow for him to thank me properly before the door closed.

For the second time in twenty-four hours I had failed to fill an order, and as I went back to where I had parked the roadster and started uptown I was in no mood to keep to the right and stop for lights. It was more than likely that Judd would get away with it. If a man in his position maintained that Cliff had either misread the license number of the car or was lying, there wasn't much the cops could or would do about it. They might have a try at the chauffeur, but of course Judd would have attended to that.

It was with the idea in mind of a substitute for Judd that I turned west on 26th Street and drove to the Tingley Building. Not something just as good, but anyhow something. But that was a dud, too. The place was silent and deserted, which I suppose was natural in view of what had happened.

I thought I might as well proceed with my search for a substitute, and, after consulting my memo book, drove to 23rd Street and turned east and stopped in front of an old brownstone. The vestibule was clean, with the brass fronts of the mailboxes polished and shining, including the one which bore the name of Yates, where I pressed the button. I entered on the click, mounted one flight, and had my finger on a button at a door in the rear when the door was opened by Gwendolyn herself.

"Oh," she said. "You."

Her face was moderately haggard, and her lids were so swollen that her eyes didn't seem anything like as keen and shrewd as they had the day before.

I asked if I could come in, and she made room for me and then led the way into a large living-room. Sitting there was Carrie Murphy. She looked as if she had been either crying or fighting; with an Irish girl you can't tell.

"You folks look kind of all in," I said sympathetically.

Miss Yates grunted. "We didn't get much sleep. They kept us up most of the night, and who could sleep, anyway?" She gazed at me curiously. "It was you that found him."

"It was," I agreed.

"What did you go there for?"

"Just to invite him to call on Nero Wolfe to discuss quinine."

"Oh. I was going to phone you. I want to see Amy Duncan. Do you know where she is?"

That made her a pushover. "Well," I said, "she spent the night up at our place under the care of a doctor. I left early this morning, so I can't guarantee that she's still there, but I suppose she is."

"The paper says," Carrie Murphy put in, "that she's going to be detained for questioning. Does that mean that she's suspected of killing her uncle?"

"Certainly."

"Then—"

"We want to see her," Miss Yates interposed.

"Okay, come along. I've got a car."

It still lacked a couple of minutes till eleven when we got there, so Wolfe hadn't come down from the plant rooms, and the office was empty. I got the visitors arranged in chairs and then beat it to the roof. Wolfe was at the sink in the potting room washing his hands.

"The baboon named Judd," I reported, "is going to have me jailed for annoying him. Probably you, too. He's the kind you read about, made of silk reinforced with steel, very tough. He has informed the police that Cliff is a liar. I went to Tingley's and found no one there. I found Miss Yates at her apartment, and Carrie

Murphy there making a call, and they said they wanted to see Amy Duncan, so I told them she was here and brought them along."

I made myself scarce before he could make what he would have regarded as a fitting comment on my failure to get Judd. On my way down I stopped at my room to powder my nose, and heard the elevator start its descent, so I hurried along.

He acted fairly human when I introduced the two callers. After ringing for beer and heaving a sigh of pleasure when Fritz brought it in, he leaned back and slanted his eyes at Gwendolyn.

"Mr. Goodwin tells me you wish to see Miss Duncan. She's not here. The police came with a warrant and took her."

"A warrant?" Carrie Murphy demanded. "Do you mean she's arrested?"

"Yes. As a material witness. They took her from my house. I don't like people being taken from my house with warrants. Her bond is being arranged for. Are you ladies friends of hers?"

"We know her," said Miss Yates. "We're not enemies. We don't want to see her unjustly accused."

"Neither do I. I think it very unlikely that she had anything to do with that quinine. What do you think?"

"The same as you do. Will they let us see her?"

"I doubt it."

"You see," Carrie blurted, "there's something we didn't tell the police! We didn't want them to know about the quinine!"

Wolfe shrugged. "That's absurd. They already know. Not only from Mr. Goodwin, from Mr. Cliff, too. What was it that you didn't tell them?"

"We didn't—" Carrie checked herself and looked at her boss. Miss Yates compressed her lips and said nothing. Carrie transferred back to Wolfe. "We don't know," she said, "whether it's important or not. From what it says in the paper we can't tell. That's what we want to ask Amy. Can we ask you?"

"Try."

"Well—Amy was there, wasn't she?"

"At the Tingley Building last evening? Yes."

"What time did she get there?"

"Five minutes past seven."

"And what happened?"

"As she entered the office someone who was hiding behind the screen hit her on the head with an iron weight and knocked her unconscious. She remained unconscious for an hour. When Mr. Goodwin arrived, at eight minutes past eight, she was trying to descend the stairs, but collapsed again. He brought her here, after investigating upstairs and finding Tingley's body. She says that when she entered the office her uncle was not in sight, so it is supposed that he was already dead."

Carrie shook her head. "He wasn't."

Wolfe's brows went up. "He wasn't?"

"No. And Amy didn't kill him."

"Indeed. Were you there?"

"Of course I wasn't there. But if she had been knocked unconscious, could she have murdered a man? Even if she would?"

"Probably not. But you are postulating that she is telling the truth. The police aren't so gallant. What if she's lying? What if someone hit her after she had killed her uncle? What if she killed him soon after her arrival?"

"Oh, no," Carrie declared triumphantly, "she couldn't! That's just it! Because we know he was alive at eight o'clock!"

Wolfe gazed at her, with his lips pushed out. Then he poured beer, drank, used his handkerchief, leaned back, and leveled his eyes at her again. "That's interesting," he murmured. "How do you know that?"

"He was talking on the telephone."

"At eight o'clock?"

"Yes."

"To you?"

"No," Miss Yates interposed. "To me. At my home. Miss Murphy was there and heard it."

"Are you sure it was Mr. Tingley?"

"Certainly. I've known him all my life."

"What were you talking about?"

Gwendolyn answered, "A private matter."

Wolfe shook his head. "The police will soon pull you off that perch, madam. It's murder. I, of course, have no authority, but, since we've gone this far . . ."

"It's about the quinine. One of the girls reported to me that she had seen Miss Murphy doing something suspicious. Yesterday afternoon, just before closing time. Sneaking some of a mix into a little jar and concealing it. I asked Miss Murphy for an explanation and she refused to give any. Told me that she had nothing to say—"

"I couldn't—"

"Let me finish, Carrie. After she had gone home I went to Mr. Tingley's office and was going to tell him about it, but I don't think he even heard what I said. I had never seen him so upset. Philip, his adopted son, had just been there, and I suppose that was it, but he didn't say anything about Philip. I left at a quarter after six and went home to my flat on Twenty-third Street. I always walk; it's only a seven minutes' walk. I took off my hat and coat and rubbers and put my umbrella in the bathtub to drain, and ate some sardines and cheese—"

She stopped, and grunted. "The police asking me

questions all night seems to have got me into a habit. I don't suppose you care what I ate. About half past seven Miss Murphy came. She said she had been thinking it over and had decided she ought to tell me about it. What she told me made me madder than I've ever been in my life. Mr. Tingley suspected me of putting that quinine in! Me!"

"That isn't fair, Miss Yates," Carrie protested. "It was only—"

"Rubbish!" Gwen snapped. "He had you spying on me, didn't he?"

"But he—"

"I say he had you spying on me!" Miss Yates turned to Wolfe. "Since this trouble started, we've kept a sharp eye on the mixers and filling benches, and I've sent a sample of every mix in to Mr. Tingley, including even Carrie's. And, behind my back, she was sending him samples of my mixes!"

"I was obeying orders," Carrie said defensively. "Could I help it?"

"No. But he could. If he were alive I'd never forgive him for that—but now—I'll try to. I've given my whole life to that factory. That's the only life I've got or ever have had, and he knew it. He knew how proud I was of every jar that left that place, and yet he could set a spy on me—"

"So," Wolfe said, "you phoned Mr. Tingley to give him the devil."

She nodded.

"How do you know it was eight o'clock?"

"Because I looked at my watch. I called his home first, but he wasn't there, so I tried the office."

"Did he corroborate Miss Murphy's story?"

"Yes. He admitted it. He didn't even apologize. He said he was the head of the business, and no one,

36

not even me, was above suspicion. He told me that to my face!"

"Not precisely to your face."

"Well, he said it!" She blew her nose again. "I hung up. I had a notion to go and have it out with him, but I decided to wait till morning. Anyway, I was played out—I had been under a strain for a month. Carrie stayed and I made some tea. I couldn't blame her, since she had only done what he told her to. We were still there talking at ten o'clock when a policeman came."

"With the news of the murder."

"Yes."

"But you didn't tell about the phone call."

"No," Miss Yates said. "I didn't want them to know about the quinine."

"But we'll have to tell them now," Carrie said. She was sitting on the edge of her chair with her fingers twisted into knots. "Since they've arrested Amy. Won't we?"

Wolfe grimaced. "Not for that reason," he said grumpily. "It would do Miss Duncan more harm than good. They think she's lying, anyhow. Do as you please. For myself, I shall tell them nothing."

They discussed it. Wolfe drank more beer. I covered a yawn, feeling that my substitute for Guthrie Judd had turned pretty sour on us. If Tingley had been alive at eight o'clock, Judd couldn't very well have killed him between 7:30 and 7:35, nor could the other man, the one in the raincoat, between 7:40 and 7:47. Of course, either of them could have returned just after eight, but, since I arrived at 8:08, that would have been cutting it fine, and besides, Cliff would have seen them unless they entered by another way. Unless Cliff was lying, or Amy was, or these two tidbit mixers were . . .

When they finally left, their intentions still appeared to be in a state of heads or tails. I offered to take them back to 23rd Street, which seemed only fair under the circumstances, and they accepted. That is, Gwendolyn did; Carrie said she was bound for the subway, so with her I went on to 34th and unloaded her at the express station.

When I got back I found that company had arrived. Leonard Cliff and Amy Duncan were there in the office with Wolfe. Cliff looked so grim and harassed. Amy was worse, if anything. She was puffy under the eyes and saggy at the jaws. The soft in-curves I had liked in her cheeks weren't there. Wolfe, himself, turned a black scowl on me.

I sat down. "My God," I said, "it could be worse, couldn't it? What if they charged you and tossed you in the coop?"

"Miss Duncan," Wolfe growled, "is under bond. The thing has become ridiculous. Mr. Cramer states that the knife handle bears her fingerprints."

"No!" I raised the brows. "Really? How about the chunk of iron? The weight."

"None. Clean."

"Ha. I thought so. She forgot to remove her prints from the knife, but after banging herself on the bean with the weight she carefully wiped it off—"

"That will do, Archie! If you insist on being whimsical—"

"I am not being whimsical. I'm merely agreeing with you that it's ridiculous." I sent him back his glare. "I know what you're doing, and so do you! You're letting it slide! Your performance with those two women I brought here was pitiful! I've got legs and I'm using them. You've got a brain and where is it? You're sore at Tingley because he got killed before you could shake your finger at him and tell him to keep quinine out of his liver pâté. You're sore at Cramer because he offended your dignity. You're sore at me because I didn't get Judd. Now you're sore at Miss Duncan because while she was lying there unconscious she let someone put her prints on that knife."

I turned to Amy: "You shouldn't permit things like that to happen. They annoy Mr. Wolfe."

Wolfe shut his eyes. There was a long silence. The tip of his forefinger was making little circles on the arm of his chair. Finally his lids went up halfway, and I was relieved to see that the focus was not me but Amy. He leaned back and clasped his fingers above his breadbasket. "Miss Duncan," he said, "it looks as if we'll have to go all over it. Are you up to answering some questions?"

"Oh, yes," she declared. "Anything that will—I feel pretty good. I'm all right."

"You don't look it. I'm going on the assumption that you and Mr. Cliff are telling the truth. I shall abandon it only under necessity. I assume, for instance, that when you left your uncle's employ and later became Mr. Cliff's secretary you were not coming to terms with the enemy."

"You certainly may," Cliff put in. "We knew she had worked in Tingley's office, but we didn't know she was his niece. That's why I was so surprised when I saw she was going there last evening, I couldn't imagine what she was doing there."

"Very well. I'll take all that." Wolfe went on with Amy: "What would you say if I told you that Miss Murphy was responsible for the quinine?"

"Why—" Amy looked astonished. "I wouldn't know what to say. I'd ask you how you knew. I couldn't believe that Carrie would do a thing like that."

"Did she have a grudge against your uncle?"

"Not that I know of. No special grudge. Of course, nobody really liked him."

"What about Miss Yates?"

"Oh, she's all right. She's a kind of a holy terror with the girls in the factory, but she's certainly competent."

"Did you and she get along?"

"Well enough. We didn't have much to do with each other. I was my uncle's stenographer."

"How were her relations with Tingley?"

"As good as could be expected. Of course, she was a privileged character; he couldn't possibly have got along without her. He inherited her from my grandfather along with the business."

Wolfe grunted. "Speaking of inheritance. Do you know anything about your uncle's will? Who will get the business?"

"I don't know, but I suppose my cousin Philip."

"His adopted son?"

"Yes." Amy hesitated, then offered an amendment by a change of inflection: "I *suppose* he will. The business has always been handed down from father to son. But, of course, Philip—" She stopped.

"Is he active in the business?"

"No. That's just it. He isn't active in anything. Except—" She stopped.

"Except—?" Wolfe prodded her.

"I was going to say, except spending money, only for the past year or so he hasn't had any to spend. Since Uncle Arthur kicked him out. I suppose he's been giving him enough to keep him from starving. I thought—I had an idea, when my uncle phoned and asked me to come to his office yesterday, and he was so urgent about it, that it was something about Philip."

"Why did you think that?"

"Well—because the only other time he ever sent for me it was about Philip. He thought that I could—that I had an influence over him."

"Did you?"

"Maybe—a little."

"When was the other time?"

"Nearly a year ago."

"What did he want you to influence Philip to do?"

"To—well, to settle down. To take an interest in the business. He knew that Philip was—had wanted to marry me. Of course, Philip isn't really my first cousin, since he was adopted. He isn't any relation at all, but I didn't want to marry him. I wasn't in love with him."

"And your uncle tried to persuade you to marry him?"

"Oh, no. He was dead against our marrying—I thought that was odd—but anyway he thought I had enough influence with Philip to reform him."

"Had Philip, himself, abandoned the idea of marrying you?"

"Well, he—he had quit trying."

Leonard Cliff was scowling. "Look here," he blurted at her suddenly, "what does he look like?"

"Philip?"

"Yes."

"Why—he's tall. Tall and broad, with a bony face and deep-set eyes. He's cynical. I mean he looks cynical—"

Cliff hit the arm of his chair with his palm. "It was him! I saw him at police headquarters this morning. It was him!"

"What if it was?" Wolfe demanded impatiently.

"Because that's what I came to tell you about! He's the man I saw last night! The one in the raincoat!"

"Indeed," Wolfe said. "The one who arrived at seven-forty? After Mr. Judd left?"

"Yes!"

"How sure are you?"

"Damned sure. I was sure when I saw him there at headquarters, and I started to try to find out who he was, but they hustled me out. And now, from the description Amy gives—"

Wolfe snapped at Amy, "Do you know where he lives?"

She shook her head. "No, I don't. But, oh—I can't believe—you don't think—"

"I haven't begun to think. First I have to get something to think about." He turned to me: "Archie, do you know of anyone we might hire to find Philip Tingley and bring—"

That was all I heard. I was on my way out.

This was the third man I had been sent for in less than twenty-four hours. The first one had been dead when I got to him. The second one had threatened to have me jailed. I intended to get this one.

But first I had to find him, and that turned into a job. From the colored maid at Tingley's house I got the address easily enough, east of Second Avenue on 29th Street, but he wasn't there. It was a dump, a dingy, dirty, five-story walk-up. I pushed the button labeled "Philip Tingley," but got no answering click. The button's position showed that he was four flights up, and since the door was unlatched, I entered and climbed the dark and smelly stairs. There were no buttons on the inside doors, so at the fifth floor rear I knocked half a dozen times, but without result.

I sat down at the top of the stairs and tried not to stew for nearly two hours.

Up to five o'clock that was one of the most unsatisfactory afternoons I remember. The sensible thing would have been to get Fred Durkin, who works for Wolfe on occasion, and leave him on post while I explored, but I wanted to make the delivery without any help. After a dish of beans and a couple of glasses of milk at a joint on Second Avenue I tried again, with the same result. Inquiries of the janitor in the basement and some of the other tenants were a good language lesson, but that was all. At half past four I went out again and did some research from a phone booth and drew nothing but blanks. It was during that expedition that he flew back to the nest. When I returned, a little after five o'clock, and, just to be doing something, pressed the button in the vestibule, the click sounded immediately. I popped in and bounced up the four flights.

The door to the rear flat was standing open and he was there on the sill when I reached his level. My first glance at him showed me not only that Amy's description had. been accurate, but that I was an unwelcome surprise. He didn't like me at all.

"What do you want?" he demanded as I appeared.

I grinned at him. "You, brother. I've been around here wanting you for five hours."

"Are you from the police?"

"Nope. My name's Goodwin. I—"

The ape was shutting the door. I got against it and slid inside.

"Get out!" he snarled. "Get out of here!"

"My goodness," I protested, "you haven't even asked me what I want! How do you know I'm not Santa Claus?" I kicked the door shut behind me. There was no hurry, since Wolfe wouldn't be available until six o'clock. "Let's go in and talk it over—"

I suppose I was careless but what he did was so unexpected that he had me before I knew it. Not only did he get his long, bony fingers around my throat, but the strength of his grip indicated that they weren't all bone. I grabbed his wrists, but that was no good; he had the leverage. I ducked and twisted, and broke his hold, but he pressed on in, clutching at me, scratching me on the cheek. I don't like to plug a guy who never learned what fists are for, but I don't like to be scratched, either, so I pushed him back with my left and hooked with my right. He staggered, but the wall kept him from going down.

"Cut it out," I said curtly. "I don't want to—"

He hauled off and kicked me! What with my throat hurting when I talked, and the scratch on my cheek, and now this, I hit him harder, the second time, than I intended to. He didn't topple over, he folded up. As if he had melted. Then he didn't move.

I stooped over for a look at him, and then slid past for an inspection of the premises. The only way I could account for his violent lack of hospitality before he ever knew what I came for was that there was someone else there who wasn't supposed to be. But the place was empty. All there was of it was a bedroom and kitchen and bath. I gave them a glimpse, including the closet and under the bed, and went back to the tenant. He was still out.

In view of his disinclination even to let me state my intentions, it didn't seem likely that I would get any kind of co-operation from him in my desire to escort him to Wolfe's house, so I decided to wrap him up. He was too big to do anything with in the narrow little hall, and I dragged him into the kitchen. With a length of old clothesline from a kitchen drawer and a roll of adhesive tape from the bathroom cabinet, I soon had him arranged so that he would at least listen to me without kicking and scratching. I was putting the third strip of tape crosswise on his mouth when a bell rang right behind me.

I jerked up. The bell rang again.

So that was it. Not that someone was there, but someone was expected. I found the button on the wall that released the door latch downstairs, pushed it several times, took a swift look at the job I had just completed, stepped out and closed the kitchen door, and opened the door to the public hall.

I heard faint and hesitating footsteps from below on the uncarpeted stairs. Before a head appeared above the landing I had decided it was a woman; and it was. When she got to my level she stopped again, glanced the other way, and then saw me. She was a new one on me. Fifty or maybe a little more, slim and slick, in a mink coat.

I said politely, "Good evening."

She asked, with a sort of gasp, "Are you—Philip Tingley?"

I nodded. "Don't you recognize me?"

That seemed to hit some mark. "How would I recognize you?" she demanded sharply.

"I don't know. From my statue in the park, maybe." I stood aside from her passage to the door. "Come in."

She hesitated a second; then pulled her shoulders up as if bracing herself against peril and swept by me. I followed her in and motioned her to the living-bedroom and shut the door. All was dark before me, figuratively speaking, but anyway I could try some fancy groping and stumbling.

I went up to her. "Let me take your coat. This isn't the sort of chair you're used to, but it'll have to do."

She shuddered away from me and glanced nervously around. When she sat she let just enough of her come in contact with the shabby, soiled upholstery to call it sitting. Then she looked at me. I have never regarded myself as a feast for the eye, my attractions run more to the spiritual, but on the other hand I am not a toad, and I resented her expression.

"It seems," I ventured, "that something about me falls short of expectations."

She made a contemptuous noise. "I told you on the phone that there can be nothing sentimental about me and never has been."

"Okay," I agreed. "I'm not sentimental, either."

"I wouldn't expect you to be." If the breath of her voice had dribbled off the edge of a roof it would have made icicles. "It's not in you from either side. Neither from your father nor from me. My brother says you're a blackguard. He also says you're a coward and a bluffer, but considering where your blood came from, I don't believe that. I tell you frankly, I think my brother is making a mistake." She was biting the words off. "That's why I came. He thinks you'll take what he has offered, but I don't. I know I wouldn't, and half of you came from me."

I was loping along behind trying to keep up. The best bet seemed to be that I was a blackguard, so I did as well as I could with a sneer. "He thinks I'm a coward, does he?" I emitted an ugly little laugh. "And he thinks I'll take his offer? I won't!"

"What will you take?"

"What I said! That's final!"

"It is not final," she said sharply. "You're making a mistake, too. You're a fool if you think my brother will give you a million dollars."

"He will, or else."

"No. He won't." She moved on the chair, and I thought she was going to slide off, but she didn't. "All men are fools," she said bitterly. "I thought I had a cool head and knew how to take care of myself, but I was doomed to be ruined by men. When I was a pretty little thing in that factory—that finished me with men, I thought—but there are more ways than one. I don't deny that you have some right to—something; but what you demand is ridiculous. What my brother offers is also ridiculous, I admit that. If I had money of my own but I haven't. You're obdurate fools, both of you. He has never learned to compromise, and apparently you haven't, either. But you'll have to on this; you both will."

I kept the sneer working. "He's a pigheaded blubber-lip," I asserted. "It takes two to compromise. How about him?"

She opened her mouth and closed it again.

"So," I said sarcastically. "It strikes me that you're not any too bright yourself. What good did you expect to do by coming here and reading me the riot act? Do you think I'm boob enough to say, okay, split the difference, and then you run back to him? Now, that would be smart, wouldn't it?"

"It would at least make—"

"No!" I stood up. "You want this settled. So do I. So does he, and I know it. All right, let's go see him together. Then you can tell both of us to compromise. Then we'll find out who's being ridiculous. Come on."

She looked startled. "You mean now?"

"I mean now."

She balked. She had objections. I overruled them. I had the advantage, and I used it. When I put on my coat she just sat and chewed on her lip. Then she got up and came along.

When we got downstairs and out to the sidewalk there was no car there but mine; apparently she had come in a cab. I doubted if Philip Tingley ought to own a car, so I snubbed it and we walked to the corner and flagged a taxi. She shoved clear into her corner and I returned the compliment, after hearing her give an address in the 70's just east of Fifth Avenue. During the ride she showed no desire for conversation.

She allowed Philip to pay the fare, which seemed to me a little scrubby, under the circumstances. Before the massive ornamental door to the vestibule she stood aside, and I depressed the lever and pushed it open. The inner door swung open without any summons, and she passed through, with me on her heels. A man in uniform closed the door.

She seemed to have shrunk, and she looked pale and peaked. She was scared stiff. She asked the man, "Is Mr. Judd upstairs?"

"Yes, Miss Judd."

She led me upstairs to a large room with a thousand books and a fireplace and exactly the kind of chairs I like. In one of them was a guy I didn't like. He turned his head at our entrance.

Her voice came from a constricted throat: "Guthrie, I thought—"

What stopped her was the blaze from his eyes. It was enough to stop anyone.

I walked over and asked him, "Is Aiken around?"

He ignored me. He spoke to his sister as if she had been a spot of grease: "Where did this man come from?"

"It's a long story," I said, "but I'll make it short. She went to Philip Tingley's flat and I was there and she thought I was him." I waved a hand. "Mistaken identity."

"She thought—" He was speechless. That alone was worth the price of admission. His sister was staring at me frozenly.

He picked on her. "Get out!" he said in cold fury. "You incomparable fool!"

She was licked. She went.

I waited till the door had closed behind her and

then said, "We had a good, long talk. It's an interesting situation. Now I can give you an invitation I was going to extend yesterday when you interrupted me. You're going down to Thirty-fifth Street to call on Nero Wolfe."

"I'll talk with you," he said between his teeth. "Sit down."

"Oh, no. I invited you first. And I don't like you. If you do any wriggling and squirming, I swear I'll sell it to a tabloid and retire on the proceeds." I pointed to the door. "This way to the egress." . . .

Wolfe sat at his desk. I sat at mine, with my notebook open. Guthrie Judd was in the witness box, near Wolfe's desk.

Wolfe emptied his beer glass, wiped his lips, and leaned back. "You don't," he said, "seem to realize that the thing is now completely beyond your control. All you can do is save us a little time, which we would be inclined to appreciate. I make no commitment. We can collect the details without you if we have to, or the police can. The police are clumsy and sometimes not too discreet, but when they're shown where to dig they do a pretty good job. We know that Philip Tingley is your sister's son, and that's the main thing. That's what you were struggling to conceal. The rest is only to fill in. Who, for instance, is Philip's father?"

Judd, his eyes narrowed, and his jaw clamped, gazed at him in silence.

"Who is Philip's father?" Wolfe repeated patiently. Judd held the pose.

Wolfe shrugged. "Very well." He turned to me. "Call Inspector Cramer. With the men he has, a thing like this— Did you make a noise, sir?"

"Yes," Judd snapped. "Damn you. Philip's father is dead. He was Thomas Tingley. Arthur's father."

"I see. Then Arthur was Philip's brother."

"Half-brother." Judd looked as if he would rather say it with bullets than words. "Thomas was married and had two children, a son and a daughter, by his wife. The son was Arthur."

"Was the wife still alive when—?"

"Yes. My sister went to work in the Tingley factory in 1909. I was then twenty-five years old, just getting a start in life. She was nineteen. Arthur was a year or two younger than me. His father, Thomas, was approaching fifty. In 1911 my sister told me she was pregnant and who was responsible for it. I was making a little more money then, and I sent her to a place in the country. In September of that year the boy was born. My sister hated him without ever seeing him. She refused to look at him. He was placed in a charity home, and was forgotten by her and me. At that time I was occupied with my own affairs to the exclusion of considerations that should have received my attention. Many years later it occurred to me that there might be records at that place which would be better destroyed, and I had inquiries made."

"When was that?"

"Only three years ago. I learned then what had happened. Thomas Tingley had died in 1913, and his wife a year later. His son Arthur had married in 1912, and Arthur's wife had died in an accident. And in 1915 Arthur had legally adopted the four-year-old boy from the charity home."

"How did you know it was that boy?"

"I went to see Arthur. He knew the boy was his half-brother. His father, on his deathbed, had told him all about it and charged him with the child's welfare—secretly, since at that time Thomas's wife was still alive. Two years later, after Arthur's wife had died, leaving him childless, he had decided on the adoption."

50

"You said you had a search made for records. Did Arthur have them?"

"Yes, but he wouldn't give them up. I tried to persuade him. I offered—an extravagant sum. He was stubborn, he didn't like me, and he was disappointed in the boy, who had turned out a blithering fool."

Wolfe grunted. "So you made efforts to get the records by other methods."

"No. I didn't." A corner of Judd's mouth twisted up. "You can't work me into a melodrama. I don't fit. Not even a murder. I knew Arthur's character and had no fear of any molestation during his life-time, and he conceded me a point. He put the papers in a locked box in his safe and willed the box and its contents to me. Not that he told me where they were. I found that out later."

"When?"

"Two days ago."

Wolfe's brows went up. "Two *days*?"

"Yes. Monday morning Philip called at my office. I had never seen him since he was a month old, but he established his identity, and he had copies with him of those records. He demanded a million dollars." Judd's voice rose. "A million!"

"What was the screw, a threat to publish?"

"Oh, no. He was smoother than that. He said he came to me only because his adopted father would allow him nothing but a pittance—he said 'pittance' —and had disinherited him in his will. Arthur had been fool enough to let him read the will, rubbing it in, I suppose, and the bequest of the locked box to me had made him smell a rat. He had stolen the box from the safe and got it open, and there it was. His threat was not to publish, but to sue me and my sister for damages, for abandoning him as an infant, which of course amounted to the same thing, but that put a face on it.

51

And was something we could not allow to happen under any circumstances, and he knew it."

Wolfe said, "So why didn't you pay him?"

"Because it was outrageous. You don't just hand out a million dollars."

"I don't, but you could."

"I didn't. And I wanted a guaranty that that would end it. For one thing I had to be sure I was getting all the original records, and Arthur was the only one who could satisfy me on that, and he would see me Monday. I put Philip off for a day. The next morning, yesterday, Arthur phoned me that the box was gone from the safe, but even then he wouldn't come to my office or meet me somewhere, so I had to go to him."

I looked up from the notebook with a grin. "Yeah, and I met you coming out. When I put that chalk—"

He rudely went on without even glancing at me. "I went to his office and told him of Philip's demand and threat. He was enraged. He thought Philip could be brow-beaten into surrendering the box, and I didn't. What I proposed—but I couldn't do anything with him. He would have it his way. It was left that he would talk with Philip that afternoon, and the three of us would have it out the next morning, Wednesday—that would have been today—in his office. I had to accept—"

"That won't do," Wolfe said bluntly. "Don't try any dodging now."

"I'm not. I am telling you—"

"A lie, Mr. Judd. It's no good. You three were to meet at Tingley's office Tuesday evening, not Wednesday morning. And you went there—"

I missed the rest. The doorbell rang, and I went to attend to it, because Fritz wasn't being permitted to exert himself. A peep through the glass showed me a phiz only too well known, so I slipped the chain on

ntered the Tingley Building at seven-thirty
evening. Do you still say that?"

taking your chauffeur down to headquarters."
made a contemptuous noise.

Philip Tingley. You might as well come down
rse. Somebody's going to talk; don't think
If you expect—"

one rang. I answered it, and learned that
ster wished to speak to Inspector Cramer.
e to my desk to take it. About all he did for
was listen and grunt. At the end he said,
here to Nero Wolfe's place," and hung up.
don't object," he said to Wolfe.
t?" Wolfe demanded.

talk with Philip Tingley. They found him
tchen tied up and gagged." . . .

ot, and always will have, a soft spot in my
p Tingley. Consider the situation from his
en he entered Nero Wolfe's office at seven
Wednesday evening. Two burly detectives
ehind him. He was surrounded by the
w was swollen, his head must have been
was wobbly on his pins. He knew I was
he was. And yet, by gum, the minute he
f me he power-dived at me as if all he
lant one bomb! That's the spirit that wins

jumped for him. I hastily arose, but they
ld him.

hell?" Cramer inquired.

ate matter," I explained, sitting down.
fixed his jaw and tied him up. That has

ny feet again. With one mighty, spas-
his bony frame Philip had busted loose

before I opened the door to the extent of the six inches
which the chain permitted.

"We don't need any," I said offensively.

"Go to hell," I was told gruffly. "I want to see
Guthrie Judd. He's here."

"How do you know?"

"So informed at his home. Take off that damn'
chain—"

"He might have got run over on the way. Be
seated while I find out."

I went to the office and told Wolfe, "Inspector
Cramer wants to see Judd. Was told at his home that he
had come here."

Judd, quick on the trigger, spoke up: "I want your
assurance."

"You won't get it," Wolfe snapped. "Bring Mr.
Cramer in."

I went back out and slipped the chain and swung
the door open, and Cramer made for the office with me
following.

After using grunts for greetings he stood and spoke
down to Judd: "This is a confidential matter. Very confidential. If you want to come—"

Judd glanced at Wolfe from the corner of his eye.
Wolfe cleared his throat.

Judd said, "Sit down. Go ahead."

"But I warn you, Mr. Judd, it is extremely—"

"He has answered you," Wolfe said. "Please make
it as brief as possible."

"I see." Cramer looked from one to the other.
"Like that, huh? Suits me." He sat down and placed
the leather bag on the floor in front of him, and hunched
over and released the catches and opened it. He straightened up to look at Judd. "A special-delivery parcel-post
package addressed to me by name was delivered at
police headquarters about an hour ago." He bent and

got an object from the bag. "This was in it. May I ask, have you ever seen it before?"

Judd said, "No."

Cramer's eyes moved. "Have you, Wolfe? You, Goodwin?"

Wolfe shook his head. I said, "Not guilty."

Cramer shrugged. "As you see, it's a metal box with a lock. On the top the letters 'GJ' have been roughly engraved, probably with the point of a knife. The first thing about it is this: A box of this description, including the 'GJ' on its top, was left to you by Arthur Tingley in his will. The police commissioner asked you about it this afternoon, and you stated you knew nothing of such a box and had no idea what it might contain. Is that correct, Mr. Judd?"

"It is," Judd acknowledged. "Hombert told me the will said the box would be found in the safe in Tingley's office, and it wasn't there."

"That's right. The second thing is the lock has been forced. It was like that when the package was opened. The third thing is the contents." Cramer regarded Judd. "Do you want me to keep right on?"

"Go ahead."

"Very well." Cramer lifted the lid.

"Item one, a pair of baby shoes." He held them up for inspection.

"Item two, a printed statement of condition of your banking firm. As of June 30, 1939. A circle has been made, with pen and ink, around your name, and a similar circle around the sum of the total resources, $230,000,000 and something."

He returned the folder to the box and produced the next exhibit. "Item three, a large manila envelope. It was sealed, but the wax has been broken and the flap slit open. On the outside, in Arthur Tingley's handwrit-

ing, is this inscription: 'C[...]
decease, to be delivered i[...]
Arthur Tingley.' "

Judd had a hand exten[...]
tone was sharp and peremp[...]

"No, sir; I didn't." C[...]
lope. "It had already been [...]
your property, and eventu[...]
rendered to you, but we[...]
Under the circumstances.[...]
cate of 'Baby Philip,' dat[...]
pages from the records [...]
garding the sojourn in tha[...]
named Martha Judd, an[...]
graph, dated July 9, 19[...]
Also, a certificate of the [...]
by Arthur Tingley, date[...]
inspect these document[...]

"No," Judd snapp[...]
surrender of the box an[...]

Cramer shook his [...]
"I'll replevy."
"I doubt if you ca[...]
"That has nothing[...]
"I hope it hasn't.[...]
it. "I'm only a cop an[...]
in your position and [...]
the district attorney [...]
job, and that's that.[...]
Was she at the Elle[...]

"It would have [...]
icily, "to follow th[...]
aimed a finger at th[...]

"Yeah, I hear[...]
know, even with y[...]

you that [...]
yesterday [...]
"Yes. [...]
"We'r[...]
Judd [...]
"Also [...]
off your ho[...]
they won't.[...]

The p[...]
Sergeant F[...]
Cramer cam[...]
two minutes[...]
"Bring him [...]
"If you [...]
"To wha[...]
"A little[...]
over in his k[...]

I have g[...]
heart for Phil[...]
standpoint w[...]
o'clock that [...]
were right b[...]
enemy. His j[...]
fuzzy, and he[...]
stronger than [...]
caught sight [...]
asked was to p[...]
ball games.

The dicks [...]
got him and he[...]
"What the[...]
"It's a priv[...]
"It was me that[...]
no bearing—"

I got on [...]
modic heave of [...]

and was on the move. But not toward me; he had changed his objective. What he was after was the metal box on Cramer's knees. He not only grabbed for it, but he got it. The dicks went for him again, this time with more fervor. One of them retrieved the box and the other one slammed him down. I went to help, and we picked him up and shoved him into a chair. Panting like a polar bear on a hot day, he glared at us, but quit trying.

"Whistle for help," Cramer said sarcastically. He looked at me. "You say you fixed his jaw? Let's take that first."

I started to explain, but Philip took the floor again, this time verbally. He had seen Judd. "You!" he yelled. "You got it! You killed him and took it! And you framed me! You had her say she was coming to see me, and you sent that man—"

"Shut up!" I told him. "Judd never sent me anywhere and never will. She did come to see you, but she saw me instead."

"He got the box!"

"You damned idiot," Judd said bitterly. "You'll cook your goose—"

"That'll do," Cramer growled. "If—"

"You can't bully me, Inspector—"

"The hell I can't. If you don't like it, go hire a lawyer. Hang onto that box, Foster." Cramer regarded Philip. "You recognize it?"

"Yes! It's mine!"

"You don't say so. When and where did you see it before?"

"I saw it when I—"

"Don't be a fool," Judd snapped. He stood up. "Come with me. I'll see you through this. Keep your mouth shut."

*   *   *

"You're too late, Mr. Judd." It was Nero Wolfe taking a hand. "Either keep still or go home. You're licked."

"I have never been licked."

"Pfui! You are now. And this is my house you're in. If you try interrupting me, Mr. Goodwin will throw you out with enthusiasm." Wolfe turned to Philip: "Mr. Tingley, I'm afraid you're holding the short end of the stick. The police have got the box. Its contents are known, so you have no lever to use on Mr. Judd. And you're deep in another hole, too. Mr. Judd, who advises you to keep your mouth shut, has himself been talking. We know of your call on him Monday and the demands you made; and of the copies you showed him of the contents of that box; and of your talk with Arthur Tingley yesterday afternoon; and of the arrangement he made for you and Mr. Judd to come to his office last evening—"

Philip snarled at Judd. "You dirty rat—"

Wolfe sailed over it. "Also, we know that you went there. You walked to the building in the rain, wearing a raincoat, entered at twenty minutes to eight, and came out again seven minutes later. What did you see inside? What did you do?"

"Don't answer him," Judd commanded sharply. "He's only—"

"Save it," Philip told him in harsh contempt. He looked sullenly at Wolfe. "Yes, I went there, and I went in, and I saw him there dead on the floor."

"What—?" Cramer began blurting, but Wolfe stopped him: "I'll do this. . . . Mr. Tingley, I beg you to reflect. I may know more than you think I do. You got there at seven-forty—is that right?"

"About that, yes."

"And Tingley was dead?"

"Yes."

58

"What if I have evidence that he was alive at eight o'clock?"

"You couldn't have. He was dead when I got there."

"Was Amy Duncan there?"

"Yes. She was on the floor unconscious."

"Did you see anyone else anywhere in the building?"

"No."

"Where did you go besides Tingley's office?"

"Nowhere. I went straight there and straight out."

"You were there seven minutes. What did you do?"

"I—" Philip halted and shifted in his chair. "I felt Amy's pulse. I wanted to get her out of there—but I didn't dare—and she was breathing all right and her pulse was pretty good. Then I—" He stopped.

"Yes? You what?"

"I looked for the box. The safe door was standing open, but it wasn't in there. I looked a few other places, and then I heard Amy move, or thought I did, and I left. Anyway, I thought Judd had been there and killed him and taken the box, so I didn't hope to find it. So I left."

Wolfe was scowling at him. "Are you aware," he demanded, "of what you're saying? Are your wits working?"

"You're damned right they are."

"Nonsense. You had previously stolen the box from the safe and had it in your possession. How could you have been looking for it in that office last evening?"

"I didn't have it in my possession."

"Oh, come. Don't be ass enough—"

"I say I didn't have it. I had had it. I didn't have it then. He went to my place and found it and took it."

"Who did? When?"

"My half-brother. Arthur Tingley. He went to my

59

flat yesterday afternoon—I don't know how he got in—and found it."

So that, I thought, turning a page of my notebook, was the errand that had called Tingley away from his office when I had gone there to interview him about quinine.

Wolfe asked, "How do you know that?"

"Because he told me. He had the box there in the safe yesterday afternoon."

"Are you telling me that at five o'clock yesterday afternoon that box was in Tingley's safe in his office?"

"I am."

"And when you returned two hours later, at seven-forty, it was gone?"

"It was. Judd had been there. Judd had taken it. And if the lousy ape thinks he can—"

"Be quiet, please," Wolfe said testily. He closed his eyes.

We sat. Wolfe's lips were moving, pushing out and then drawing in again. Judd started to say something, and Cramer shushed him. The inspector knew the signs as well as I did.

Wolfe's eyes opened, but they were directed, not at Judd or Philip, but at me. "What time," he asked, "did it begin raining yesterday?"

I said, "Seven P.M."

"Seven precisely?"

"Maybe a little after. Not much."

"Not even a drizzle before that?"

"No."

"Good." He wiggled a finger at Sergeant Foster. "Let me have that box."

Foster handed him the box.

Wolfe looked at Philip Tingley: "When you stole this from the safe you had no key for it. So you had to pry it open?"

"No," Philip denied, "I didn't pry it open."

"The metal is gouged and twisted—"

"I can't help that. I didn't do it. I suppose Judd did. I took it to a locksmith and told him I had lost my key, and had him make one that would open it."

"Then it was locked yesterday afternoon?"

"Yes."

"Good." Wolfe looked pleased with himself. "That settles it, I think. Let's see." Whereupon he grasped the box firmly in both hands and shook it violently from side to side. His attitude suggested that he was listening for something, but the banging of the shoes against the metal sides of the box was all there was to hear. He nodded with satisfaction. "That's fine," he declared.

"Nuts," Cramer said.

"By no means. Some day, Mr. Cramer—but no, I suppose never. I would like a few words with you and Archie. If your men will take these gentlemen to the front room?"

When they were shut off by the sound-proofed door Cramer advanced on Wolfe with his jaw leading the way. "Look here—"

"No," Wolfe said decisively. "I tolerate your presence here and that's all. Take a guest from my house with a warrant, will you? I want to know what has been removed from Mr. Tingley's office."

"But if Judd—"

"No. Take them if you want to, get them out of here, and I'll proceed alone."

"Do you know who killed Tingley?"

"Certainly. I know all about it. But I need something. What has been removed from that office?"

Cramer heaved a sigh. "Damn you, anyway. The corpse. Two bloody towels. The knife and the weight. Five small jars with some stuff in them which we found in a drawer of Tingley's desk. We had the stuff analyzed and it contained no quinine. We were told they were routine samples."

"That's all?"

"Yes."

"No other sample jars were found?"

"No."

"Then it's still there. It ought to be. It must be. . . . Archie, go and get it. Find it and bring it here. Mr. Cramer will telephone his men there to help you."

"Huh," Cramer grunted. "I will?"

"Certainly you will."

"As for me," I put in, "I'm a wonder at finding things, but I get better results when I know what I'm looking for."

"Pfui! What was it I spit out yesterday at lunch?"

"Oh, is that it? Okay." I beat it, then.

It was only a three-minute ride to Tingley's, and I figured it might take longer than that for Wolfe to get Cramer to make the phone call, so I took a taxi to East 29th Street and picked up the roadster and drove it on from there. The entrance door at the top of the stone steps was locked, but just as I was lifting my fist to beat a tattoo I heard the chatter of feet inside, and in a moment the door opened and a towering specimen looked down at me.

"You Goodwin?" he demanded.

"I am Mr. Goodwin. Old Lady Cramer—"

"Yeah. You sound like what I've heard of you. Enter."

I did so, and preceded him up the stairs. In Tingley's office an affair with a thin little mouth in a big face was awaiting us, seated at a table littered with newspapers.

"You fellows are to help me," I stated.

"Okay," the one at the table said superciliously.

"We'd just as soon have the exercise. But Bowen did this room. If you think you can find a button after Bowen—"

"That will do, my man," I said graciously. "Bowen's all right as far as he goes, but he lacks subtlety. He's too scientific. He uses rules and calipers, whereas I use my brain. For instance, since he did that desk, it's a hundred to one that there's not an inch of it unaccounted for, but what if he neglected to look in that hat?" I pointed to Tingley's hat still there on the hook. "He might have, because there's nothing scientific about searching a hat; you just take it down and look at it."

"That's wonderful." Thin Mouth said. "Explain some more."

"Sure; glad to." I walked across. "Do you ask why Tingley would put an object in his hat? It was the logical place for it. He wanted to take it home with him, and meanwhile he wanted to keep it hidden from someone who might have gone snooping around his desk and other obvious places. He was not an obvious man. Neither am I." I reached up and took the hat from the hook.

And it was in the hat!

That made up for all the bad breaks that had come my way over a period of years. Nothing like that will ever happen again. It was so utterly unexpected that I nearly dropped it when it rolled out of the hat, but I grabbed and caught it and had it—a midget-sized jar, the kind they used for samples in the factory. It was about two thirds full with a label on it marked in pencil, "11–14–Y."

"You see," I said, trying my damnedest not to let my voice tremble with excitement, "it's a question of brains."

They were gawking at me, absolutely speechless. I

got out my penknife and, with a tip of a blade, dug out
a bit of the stuff in the jar and conveyed it to my mouth.
My God, it tasted sweet—I mean bitter!

I spat it out. "I'm going to promote you boys," I
said indulgently. "And raise your pay. And give you a
month's vacation."

I departed. I hadn't even taken off my coat and
hat. . . .

It was too bad dinner had to be delayed the first
day that Fritz was back on the job after his grippe, but
it couldn't be helped. While we were waiting for Carrie
Murphy to come, I went to the kitchen and had a glass
of milk and tried to cheer Fritz up by telling him that
grippe often leaves people so that they can't taste
anything.

At half past seven Wolfe was at his desk and I was
at mine with my notebook. Seated near me, with a dick
behind his chair, was Philip Tingley. Beyond him were
Carrie Murphy, Miss Yates, and another dick. Inspector Cramer was at the other end of Wolfe's desk, next
to Guthrie Judd. None of them looked very happy,
Carrie in particular. It was her Wolfe started on, after
Cramer had turned the meeting over to him.

"There shouldn't be much in this," Wolfe said
bluntly. What he meant was he hoped there wouldn't
be, that close to dinnertime. "Miss Murphy, did you go
to Miss Yates's apartment yesterday evening to discuss
something with her?"

Carrie nodded.

"Did she make a telephone call?"

"Yes."

"Whom did she call and at what time?"

"Mr. Arthur Tingley. It was eight o'clock."

"At his home or his office?"

"His office." She stopped to swallow. "She tried

his home first, but he wasn't there, so she called the office and got him."

"She talked with him?"

"Yes."

"Did you?"

"No."

Wolfe's eyes moved: "Miss Yates. Is Miss Murphy's statement correct?".

"It is," said Gwendolyn firmly.

"You recognized Tingley's voice?"

"Certainly. I've been hearing it all my life—"

"Of course you have. Thanks." Wolfe shifted again. "Mr. Philip Tingley. Yesterday afternoon your father—your father—your brother asked you to be at his office at seven-thirty in the evening. Is that right?"

"Yes!" Philip said aggressively.

"Did you go?"

"Yes, but not at seven-thirty. I was ten minutes late."

"Did you see him?"

"I saw him dead. On the floor behind the screen. I saw Amy Duncan there, too, unconscious, and I felt her pulse and—"

"Naturally. Being human, you displayed humanity." Wolfe made a face. "Are you sure Arthur Tingley was dead?"

Philip grunted. "If you had seen him—"

"His throat had been cut?"

"Yes, and the blood had spread—"

"Thank you," Wolfe said curtly. "Mr. Guthrie Judd."

The two pairs of eyes met in midair.

Wolfe wiggled a finger at him. "Well, sir, it looks as if you'll have to referee this. Miss Yates says Tingley was alive at eight o'clock and Philip says he was dead at seven-forty. We'd like to hear from you what shape he was in at seven-thirty. Will you tell us?"

"No."

"If you don't you're an ass. The screws are all loose now. There is still a chance this business will be censored for the press if I feel like being discreet. But I'm not bound, as law officers are, to protect the embarrassing secrets of prominent people from the public curiosity. I'm doing a job and you can help me out a little. If you don't—" Wolfe shrugged.

Judd breathed through his nose.

"Well?" Wolfe asked impatiently.

"Tingley was dead." Judd bit it off.

"Then you did enter that building and go to that office? At half past seven?"

"Yes. That was the time of the appointment. Tingley was on the floor with his throat cut. Near him was a young woman I had never seen, unconscious. I was in the room less than a minute."

Wolfe nodded. "I'm not a policeman, and I'm certainly not the district attorney, but I think it is quite likely that you will never be under the necessity of telling this story in a courtroom. They won't want to inconvenience you. However, in the event that a subpoena takes you to the witness stand, are you prepared to swear to the truth of what you have just said?"

"I am."

"Good." Wolfe's gaze swept to Miss Yates. "Are you still positive it was Tingley you talked to, Miss Yates?"

She met his eyes squarely. "I am." Her voice was perfectly controlled. "I don't say they're lying. I don't know. I only know if it was someone imitating Arthur Tingley's voice, I've never heard anything to equal it."

"You still think it was he?"

"I do."

66

"Why did you tell me this morning that when you got home yesterday you stood your umbrella in the bathtub to drain?"

"Because I—"

She stopped, and it was easy to tell from her face what had happened. An alarm had sounded inside her. Something had yelled at her, "Look out!"

"Why," she asked, her voice a shade thinner than it had been, but quite composed, "did I say that? I don't remember it."

"I do," Wolfe declared. "The reason I bring it up, you also told me you went home at a quarter past six. It didn't start raining until seven, so why did your umbrella need draining at six-fifteen?"

Miss Yates snorted. "What you remember," she said sarcastically. "What you say I said, that I didn't say—"

"Very well. We won't argue it. There are two possible explanations. One, that your umbrella got wet without any rain. Two, that you went home, not at six-fifteen, as you said you did, but considerably later. I like the second one best because it fits so well into the only satisfactory theory of the murder of Arthur Tingley. If you had gone home at six-fifteen, as you said, you wouldn't very well have been at the office to knock Miss Duncan on the head when she arrived at ten minutes past seven. Of course, you could have gone and returned to the office, but that wouldn't change things any."

Miss Yates smiled. That was a mistake, because the muscles around her mouth weren't under control, so they twitched. The result was that instead of looking confident and contemptuous she merely looked sick.

"The theory starts back a few weeks," Wolfe resumed. "As you remarked this morning, that business and that place were everything to you; you had no life except there. When the Provisions & Beverages Corporation made an offer to buy the business, you became alarmed, and upon reflection you were convinced that sooner or later Tingley would sell. That old factory would of course be abandoned, and probably you with it. That was intolerable to you. You considered ways of preventing it, and what you hit on was adulterating the product, damaging its reputation sufficiently so that the Provisions & Beverages Corporation wouldn't want it. You chose what seemed to you the lesser of two evils. Doubtless you thought that the reputation could be gradually re-established."

Carrie was staring at her boss in amazement.

"It seemed probable," Wolfe conceded, "that it would work. The only trouble was, you were overconfident. You were, in your own mind, so completely identified with the success and very existence of that place and what went on there, that you never dreamed that Tingley would arrange to check on you secretly. Yesterday afternoon you learned about it when you caught Miss Murphy with a sample of a mix you had made. And you had no time to consider the situation, to do anything about it, for a sample had already reached Tingley. He kept you waiting in the factory until after Philip had gone and he phoned his niece—for obviously you didn't know he had done that—and then called you into his office and accused you."

"It's a lie," Miss Yates said harshly. "It's a lie! He didn't accuse me! He didn't—!"

"Pfui! He not only accused you, he told you that he had proof. A jar that Miss Murphy had previously delivered to him that afternoon, from a mix you had made. I suppose he fired you. He may have told you he intended to prosecute. And I suppose you implored him, pleaded with him, and were still pleading with him, from behind, while he was stooping over the washbasin. He didn't know you had got the paperweight from his desk, and never did know it. It knocked him out. You went and got a knife and finished the job, there where he lay on the floor, and you were searching the room, looking for the sample jar which he had got from Miss Murphy, when you heard footsteps."

A choking noise came from her throat.

"Naturally, that alarmed you," Wolfe continued. "But the steps were of only one person, and that a woman. So you stood behind the screen with the weight in your hand, hoping that, whoever it was, she would come straight to that room and enter it, and she did. As she passed the edge of the screen, you struck. Then you got an idea upon which you immediately acted by pressing her fingers around the knife handle, from which, of course, your own prints had been wiped—"

A stifled gasp of horror from Carrie Murphy interrupted him. He answered it without moving his eyes from Miss Yates: "I doubt if you had a notion of incriminating Miss Duncan. You probably calculated—and for an impromptu and rapid calculation under stress is was a good one—that when it was found that the weight had been wiped and the knife handle had not, the inference would be, not that Miss Duncan had killed Tingley, but that the murderer had clumsily tried to pin it on her. That would tend to divert suspicions from you, for you had been on friendly terms with her and bore her no grudge. It was a very pretty finesse for a hasty one. Hasty, because you were now in a panic and had not found the jar. I suppose you had previously found that the safe door was open and had looked in there, but now you tried it again. No jar was visible, but a locked metal box was there on the shelf. You picked it up and shook it, and it sounded as if the jar were in it."

Cramer growled, "I'll be damned."

"Or," Wolfe went on, "it sounded enough like it to satisfy you. The box was locked. To go to the factory again and get something to pry it open with—no. Enough. Besides, the jar was in no other likely place, so that must be it. You fled. You took the box and went, leaving by a rear exit, for there might be someone in front—a car, waiting for Miss Duncan. You hurried home through the rain, for it was certainly raining then, and had just got your umbrella stood in the tub and your things off when Miss Murphy arrived."

"No!" Carrie Murphy blurted.

Wolfe frowned at her. "Why not?"

"Because she—she was—"

"Dry and composed and herself? I suppose so. An exceptionally cool and competent head has for thirty years been content to busy itself with tidbits." Wolfe's gaze was still on Miss Yates. "While you were talking with Miss Murphy you had an idea. You would lead the conversation to a point where a phone call to Tingley would be appropriate, and you did so; and you called his home first and then his office, and faked conversation with him. The idea itself was fairly clever, but your follow-up was brilliant. You didn't mention it to the police and advised Miss Murphy not to, realizing it would backfire if someone entered the office or Miss Duncan regained consciousness before eight o'clock. If it turned out that someone had, and Miss Murphy blabbed about the phone call, you could say that you had been deceived by someone imitating Tingley's voice, or even that you had faked the phone call for its effect on Miss Murphy; if it turned out that someone hadn't, the phone call would stick, with Miss Murphy to corroborate it."

A grunt of impatience came from Cramer.

"Not much more," Wolfe said. "But you couldn't open the box with Miss Murphy there. And then the police came. That must have been a bad time for you. As soon as you got a chance you forced the lid open, and I can imagine your disappointment and dismay when you saw no jar. Only a pair of child's shoes and an envelope! You were in a hole, and in your desperation you did something extremely stupid. Of course, you didn't want the box in your flat, you wanted to get rid of it, but why the devil did you mail it to Mr. Cramer? Why didn't you put something heavy in it and throw it in the river? I suppose you examined the contents of the envelope, and figured that if the police got hold of it their attention would be directed to Guthrie Judd and Philip. You must have been out of your mind. Instead of directing suspicions against Philip or Judd, the result was just the opposite, for it was obvious that neither of them would have mailed the box to the police, and therefore some other person had somehow got it."

Gwendolyn Yates was sitting straight and stiff. She was getting a hold on herself, and doing a fairly good job of it. There were no more inarticulate noises from her throat, and she wasn't shouting about lies and wasn't going to. She was a tough baby and she was tightening up.

"But you're not out of your mind now," Wolfe said, with a note of admiration in his tone. "You're adding it up, aren't you? You are realizing that I can prove little or nothing of what I've said. I can't prove what Tingley said to you yesterday, or what time you left there, or that you got the box from the safe and took it with you, or that it was you who mailed it to Mr. Cramer. I can't even prove that there wasn't someone there at eight

71

o'clock who imitated Tingley's voice over the telephone. I can't prove anything."

"Except this." He shoved his chair back, opened a drawer of his desk, and got something, arose, walked around the end of the desk, and displayed the object in front of Carrie Murphy's eyes.

"Please look at this carefully, Miss Murphy. As you see, it is a small jar two-thirds full of something. Pasted on it is a plain white label bearing the notation in pencil, 'Eleven dash fourteen dash Y.' Does that mean anything to you? Does that 'Y' stand for Yates? Look at it—"

But Carrie had no chance to give it a thorough inspection, let alone pronounce a verdict. The figure of Miss Yates, from eight feet away, came hurtling through the air. She uttered no sound, but flung herself with such unexpected speed and force that the fingers of her outstretched hand, missing what they were after, nearly poked Wolfe's eye out. He grabbed for her wrist but missed it, and then the dick was out of his chair and had her. He got her from behind by her upper arms and had her locked.

She stood, not trying to struggle, looked at Wolfe, who had backed away, and squeaked at him, "Where was it?"

He told her. . . .

We were sitting down to a dinner that was worthy of the name when the doorbell rang. I went to answer it.

The pair that entered certainly needed a tonic. Leonard Cliff looked like something peeking out at you from a dark cave. Amy Duncan was pale and puffy, with bloodshot eyes.

"We've got to see Mr. Wolfe," Cliff stated. "We've just been talking with a lawyer, and he says—"

"Not interested," I said brusquely. "Wolfe's out of the case. Through. Done."

Amy gasped. Cliff grabbed my arm. "He can't be! He can't! Where is he?"

"Eating dinner. And, by the way. I've been trying to get you folks on the phone. Some news for you. Miss Yates is under arrest: they just took her away from here. Mr. Wolfe would like to have her prosecuted for feeding him quinine, but the cops prefer to try her for murder. She's guilty of both."

"What!"

"What!"

"Yep." I waved airily. "I got the evidence. It's all over. You won't get your pictures in the paper anymore."

"You mean—she—they—it—we—"

"That's one way of putting it. I mean, the operation has been brought to a successful conclusion. You're just ordinary citizens again."

They stared at me, and then at each other, and then went into a clinch. The condition they were both in, it certainly couldn't have been merely physical attraction. I stood and regarded them patiently. Pretty soon I cleared my throat. They didn't pay any attention.

"When you get tired standing up," I said, "there's a chair in the office that will hold two. We'll join you after dinner."

I returned to help Wolfe with the snipe fired with brandy.

FRAME-UP
FOR MURDER

I

I was tailing a man mamed Jonas Putz. You can forget
Putz. I mention him only to explain how I happened to
be standing, at five o'clock that Monday afternoon, in a
doorway on the uptown side of 38th Street around the
corner from Lexington Avenue. After spending an hour
or so at the Tulip Bar of the Churchill, with an eye on
Putz at a proper distance, I had followed him out to the
street and then downtown, on foot; and after a few
blocks I got the notion that someone else was also
interested in his movements. When he stopped a couple of times to look at shop windows, I stopped, too,
naturally, and so did someone else, about twenty paces
back of me. I had first noticed her in the lobby of the
Churchill, because she rated a glance as a matter of
principle—the principle that a man owes it to his eyes
to let them rest on attractive objects when there are
any around.

She was still tagging along when I turned the corner at 38th Street, and I was wondering whether her interest in Putz had any connection with the simple little problem Nero Wolfe had been hired to solve; and, if so, what. When Putz crossed Madison Avenue and went on to the entrance of the building he lived in, and entered, I was through with him for the day, since he hadn't gone to a certain address, and it was only out of curiosity, to see what the female stalker would do, that I kept going and posted myself in a doorway across the street from Putz's entrance. My curiosity was soon satisfied.

She came right along straight to my post, stopped, faced me at arm's length, and spoke. "You are Archie Goodwin."

I raised my brows. "Prove it."

She smiled a little. "Oh, I have seen you once, at the Flamingo, and I have seen your picture in the paper. Are you detecting somebody?"

She looked about as foreign as she sounded—enough to suggest a different flavor, which can broaden a man, but not enough to make it seem too complicated. Her chin was slightly more pointed than I would have specified if I had had her made to order, but everybody makes mistakes. Her floppy-brimmed hat and the shoulder spread of her mink stole made her face look smaller than it probably was.

She wasn't an operative, that was sure. Her interest in Putz must be personal, but still it might be connected with our client's problem.

I smiled back at her. "Apparently we both are. Unless you're Putz's bodyguard?"

"Putz? Who is that?"

"Now, really. You spoke first. Jonas Putz. You ought to know his name, since you tailed him all the way here from the Churchill."

She shook her head. "Not him. I was after you. This is a pickup. I am picking you up." She didn't say "picking," but neither did she say "peecking." It was in between.

"I am honored," I assured her. "I am flattered. I like the way you do it. Usually girls who pick me up beat around the bush. Look; if you'll tell me why you're interested in Putz, I'll tell you why I am, and then we'll see. We might—"

"But I'm not! I never heard of him. Truly!" She started a hand out to touch my arm, but decided not to. "It is you I am interested in! When I saw you at the Churchill I wanted to speak, but you were going, and I followed, and all the way I was bringing up my courage. To pick you up." That time it was "peeck."

"O.K." I decided to table Putz temporarily. "Now that you've picked me up, what are you going to do with me?"

She smiled. "Oh, no. You are the man. What we do, that is for you to say."

If she had been something commonplace like a glamorous movie star I would have shown her what I thought of her passing the buck like that by marching off. If I had been busy I might have asked her for her phone number. As it was, I merely cocked my head at her.

"Typical," I said. "Invade a man's privacy and then put the burden on him. Let's see. Surely we can kill time together somehow. Are you any good at pool?"

"*Poule?* The chicken?"

"No, the game. Balls on a table and you poke them with a stick."

"Oh, the billiards. No."

"How about shoplifting? There's a shop nearby and I need some socks. There's room for a dozen pairs in that pocketbook, and I'll cover the clerk."

She didn't bat an eye. "Wool or cotton?"

"Cotton. No synthetics."

"What colors?"

"Mauve. Pinkish mauve." If I have given the impression that her chin was pointed enough to be objectionable, I exaggerated. "But we ought to plan it properly. For instance, if I have to shoot the clerk, we should separate, you can pick me up later. Let's go around the corner to Martucci's and discuss it."

She approved of that. Walking beside her, I noted that the top of the floppy-brimmed hat was at my ear level. With it off, her hair would have grazed my chin if she had been close enough. At Martucci's the crowd wouldn't be showing for another quarter of an hour, and there was an empty table in a rear corner. She asked for vermouth frappé, which was wholesome, but not very appropriate for a shoplifting moll. I told her so.

"Also," I added, "since I don't know your name, we'll have to give you one. Slickeroo Sal? Too hissy, maybe. Fanny the Finger? That has character."

"Or it could be Flora the Finger," she suggested. "That would be better because my name is Flora. Flora Gallant. Miss Flora Gallant."

"The 'Miss' is fine," I assured her. "I don't mind shooting a clerk, but I would hate to have to shoot a husband. I've heard of someone named Gallant—has a place somewhere in the Fifties. Any relation?"

"Yes," she said, "I'm his sister."

That changed things some. It had been obvious that she was no doxy. Now that she was placed, some of the tang was gone. One of the main drawbacks of marriage is that a man knows exactly who his wife is; there's not a chance that she is going to turn out to be a runaway from a sultan's harem or the Queen of the Fairies. A female friend of mine had told me things about Alec Gallant. He was a dress designer who was crowding two others for top ranking in the world of high fashion. He thumbed his nose at Paris and sneered at Rome and Ireland, and was getting away with it. He had refused to finish three dresses for the Duchess of Harwynd because she postponed flying over from London for fittings. He declined to make anything whatever for a certain famous movie actress because he didn't like the way she handled her hips when she walked. He had been known to charge as little as $800 for an afternoon frock, but it had been for a favorite customer, so he practically gave it away.

I looked at his sister over the rim of my glass as I took a sip, not vermouth, and lowered the glass. "You must come clean with me, Finger. You are Alec Gallant's sister?"

"But yes! I wouldn't try lying to Archie Goodwin. You are too smart."

"Thank you. It's too bad your brother doesn't sell socks; we could pinch them at his place instead of imposing on a stranger. Or maybe he does. Does he sell socks?"

"Good heavens, no!"

"Then that's out. As a matter of fact, I'm getting cold feet. If you're a shopkeeper's sister, you probably have a resistance to shoplifting somewhere in your subconscious, and it might pop up at a vital moment. We'll try something else. Go back to the beginning. Why did you pick me up?"

She fluttered a little hand. "Because I wanted to meet you."

"Why did you want to meet me?"

"Because I wanted you to like me."

"All right, I like you. That's accomplished. Now what?"

She frowned. "You are so blunt. You are angry with me. Did I say something?"

"Not a thing. I still like you, so far. But if you are Miss Flora Gallant you must have followed me all the way from the Churchill for one of two reasons. One would be that the sight of me was too much for you, that you were so enchanted that you lost all control. I reject that because I'm wearing a brown suit, and I get that effect only when I'm wearing a gray one. The other would be that you want something, and I ask you bluntly what it is, so we can dispose of that and then maybe go on from there. Let's have it, Finger."

"You are smart," she said. "You do like me?"

"So far, I do. I could tell better if that hat didn't shade your eyes so much."

She removed the hat, no fussing with it, and put it on a chair, and actually didn't pat around at her hair. "There," she said, "then I'll be blunt too. I want you to help me. I want to see Mr. Nero Wolfe."

I nodded. "I suspected that was it. I don't want to be rude, I am enjoying meeting you, but why didn't you just phone for an appointment?"

"Because I didn't dare. Anyway, I didn't really decide to until I saw you at the Churchill and I thought there was my chance. You see, there are three things. The first thing is that I know he charges very big fees, and I am not so rich. The second thing is that he doesn't like women, so there would be that against me. The third thing is that when people want to hire him, you always look them up and find out all you can about them, and I was afraid my brother would find out that I had gone to him, and my brother mustn't know about it. So the only way was to get you to help me, because you can make Mr. Wolfe do anything you want him to. Of course, now I've spoiled it."

"Spoiled it how?"

"By letting you pull it out of me. I was going to get friendly with you first. I know you like to dance, and I am not too bad at dancing. I would be all right with you—I know, because I saw you at the Flamingo. I thought I would have one advantage: being French I would be different from all your American girls; I know you have thousands of them. I thought in a week or two you might like me well enough so I could ask you to help me. Now I have spoiled it." She picked up her glass and drank.

I waited until she had put her glass down. "A couple of corrections. I haven't got thousands of American girls, only three or four hundred. I can't make Mr. Wolfe do anything I want him to; it all depends. And a couple of questions? What you want him to do—does it involve any marital problems? Your brother's wife or someone else's wife that he's friendly with?"

"No. My brother isn't married."

"Good. For Mr. Wolfe that would be out. You say you're not so rich. Could you pay anything at all? Could you scrape up a few hundred without hocking that stole?"

"Yes. Oh, yes. I am not a *pauvre*—pardon—a pauper. But Mr. Wolfe would sneer at a few hundred."

"That would be his impulse, but impulses can be sidetracked, with luck. I suggest that you proceed with your plan as outlined." I looked at my wrist. "It's going on six o'clock. For the Flamingo we would have to go home and dress, and that's too much trouble, but there's nothing wrong with the band at Colonna's in the Village. We can stick here for an hour or so and get acquainted, and you can give me some idea of what your problem is, and you can go right ahead with your program, getting me to like you enough to want to help you. Then we can to to Colonna's and eat and dance. Well?"

"That's all right," she conceded, "but I ought to go home and change. I would look better and dance better."

I objected. "That can come later. We'll start at the bottom and work up. If you dress, I'll have to, too, and I'd rather not. As you probably know, I live in Mr. Wolfe's house, and he might want to discuss something with me. He often does. I would rather phone and tell him I have a personal matter to attend to and won't be home for dinner. You passed the buck. You said I'm the man and it's for me to say."

"Well, I would have to phone too."

"We can afford it." I got a dime from a pocket and proffered it.

At ten-thirty the next morning, Tuesday, I was in the office on the first floor of the old brownstone on West 35th Street which is owned and dominated by Nero Wolfe, when I remembered something I had forgotten to do. Closing the file drawer I was working on, I went to the hall, turned left, and entered the kitchen, where Fritz Brenner, chef and housekeeper, was stirring something in a bowl.

I spoke. "I meant to ask, Fritz: What did Mr. Wolfe have for breakfast?"

His pink, good-natured face turned to me, but he didn't stop stirring. "Why? Something wrong?"

"Of course not. Nothing is ever wrong. I'm going to jostle him and it will help to know what mood he's in."

"A good one. He was very cheerful when I went up for the tray, which was empty. He had melon, eggs *à la Suisse* with oatmeal cakes and *croissants* with blackberry jam. He didn't put cream in his coffee, which is always a good sign. Do you have to jostle him?"

I said it was for his own good—that is, Wolfe's—

and headed for the stairs. There is an elevator, but I seldom bother to use it. One flight up was Wolfe's room, and a spare, used mostly for storage. Two flights up was my room, and one for guests, not used much. Mounting the third flight, I passed through the vestibule to the door to the plant rooms, opened it and entered.

By then, after the years, you might think those ten thousand orchids would no longer impress me, but they did. In the tropical room I took the side aisle for a look at the pink Vanda that Wolfe had been offered six grand for, and in the intermediate room I slowed down as I passed a bench of my favorites, Miltonia hybrids. Then on through to the potting room.

The little guy with a pug nose, opening a bale of osmundine over by the wall, was Theodore Horstmann, orchid nurse. The one standing at the big bench, inspecting a seed pod, was my employer.

"Good morning," I said brightly. "Fred phoned in at ten-fourteen. Putz is at his office, probably reading the morning mail. I told Fred to stay on him."

"Well?"

I'll translate it. What that "well" meant was, "You know better than to interrupt me here for that, so what is it?"

Having translated it, I replied to it, "I was straightening up a file when I suddenly realized that I hadn't told you that there's an appointment for eleven o'clock. A prospective client, someone I ran across yesterday. It might be quite interesting."

"Who is it?"

"I admit it's a woman. Her name is Flora Gallant; she's the sister of a man named Alec Gallant, who makes dresses for duchesses that dukes pay a thousand bucks for. She could get things for your wife wholesale if you had a wife."

He put the seed pod down. "Archie."

"Yes, sir."

"You are being transparent deliberately. You did not suddenly realize that you hadn't told me. You willfully delayed telling me until it is too late to notify her not to come. How old is she?"

"Oh, middle twenties."

"Of course. Ill-favored? Ill-shaped? Ungainly?"

"No, not exactly."

"She wouldn't be if you ran across her. What does she want?"

"It's a little vague. I'd rather she told you."

He snorted. "One of your functions is to learn what people want. You are trying to dragoon me. I won't see her. I'll come down later. Let me know when she has gone."

"Yes, sir." I was apologetic, "You're absolutely right. You'd probably be wasting your time. But when I was dancing with her last evening I must have got sentimental, because I told her I would help her with her problem. So I'm stuck. I'll have to tackle it myself. I'll have to take a leave of absence without pay, starting now. Say a couple of weeks, that should do it. We have nothing important on, and of course Fred can attend to Putz, and if you—"

"Archie, this is beyond tolerance. This is egregious."

"I know it is, but I'm stuck. If I were you I'd fire me. It may take—"

The house phone buzzed. He didn't move, so I went and got it. After listening to Fritz, I told him to hold on, and turned: "She's at the door. If she comes in, it will disrupt your schedule, so I'd better go down and take her somewhere. I'll—"

"Confound you," he growled. "I'll be down shortly."

I told Fritz to put her in the office and I would be right down, hung up and went. On my way through the intermediate room I cut off a raceme of Miltonia and took it along. Orchids are good for girls, whether they have problems or not. At the bottom of the stairs, Fritz was posted on guard, awaiting me. He is by no means a woman hater, but he suspects every female who enters the house of having designs on his kitchen and therefore needing to be watched. I told him O.K., I'd see to her, and crossed to the office.

She was in the red leather chair facing the end of Wolfe's desk. I told her good morning, went and got a pin from my desk tray and returned to her.

"Here," I said, handing her the raceme and pin. "I see why you asked me what his favorite color is. He'll like that dress if he's not too grouchy to notice it."

"Then he'll see me?"

"Yeah, he'll see you, any minute now. I had to back him into a corner and stick a spear in him. I doubt if I like you that much, but my honor was at stake, and I—well, if you insist—"

She was on her feet, putting her palms on my cheeks and giving me an emphatic kiss.

Since it was in the office and during hours, I merely accepted it.

"You should have another one," she said, sitting again, "for the orchids. They're lovely."

I told her to save it for a better occasion. "And," I added, "don't try it on Mr. Wolfe. He might bite you." The sound of the elevator, creaking under his seventh of a ton, came from the hall. "Here he comes. Don't offer him a hand. He doesn't like to shake hands even with men, let alone women."

There was the sound of the elevator door opening, and footsteps, and he entered. He thinks he believes in civility, so he stopped in front of her, told her good morning, and then proceeded to the over-sized, custom-made chair behind his desk.

"Your name is Flora Gallant?" he growled. The growl implied that he strongly doubted it and wouldn't be surprised if she had no name at all.

She smiled at him. I should have warned her to go slow on smiles. "Yes, Mr. Wolfe. I suppose Mr. Goodwin has told you who I am. I know I'm being nervy to expect you to take any time for my troubles—a man as busy and important as you are—but, you see, it's not for myself. I'm not anybody, but you know who my brother is? My brother Alec?"

"Yes. Mr. Goodwin has informed me. An illustrious dressmaker."

"He is not merely a dressmaker. He is an artist—a great artist." She wasn't arguing, just stating a fact. "The trouble is about him, and that's why I must be careful with it. That's why I came to you—not only that you are a great detective—the very greatest, of course; everybody knows that—but also that you are a gentleman. So I know you are worthy of confidence."

She stopped, apparently for acknowledgment. Wolfe obliged her: "Umph." I was thinking that I might also have warned her not to spread the butter too thick.

She resumed, "So it is understood I am trusting you?"

"You may," he growled.

She hesitated, seeming to consider if that point was properly covered, and decided that it was. "Then I'll tell you. I must explain that in France, where my brother and I were born and brought up, our name was not 'Gallant.' What it was doesn't matter. I have been in this country only four years. Alec came here in 1946, more than a year after the war ended. He had changed his name to Gallant and entered legally under that name. Within five years he had made a reputation as a designer, and then—I don't suppose you remember his fall collection in 1953?"

Wolfe merely grunted.

She fluttered a little hand. "But of course you are not married, and feeling as you do about women—" She let that hang. "Anyway, that collection showed everybody what my brother was—a creator, a true creator. He got financial backing, more than he needed, and opened his place on Fifty-fourth Street. That was when he sent for me to come to America, and I was glad to. From 1953 on, it has been all a triumph—many triumphs. Of course I have not had any hand in them, but I have been with him and have tried to help in my little way. The glory of great success has been my brother's, but then, he can't do everything in an affair so big as that. You understand?"

"No one can do everything," Wolfe conceded.

She nodded. "Even you, you have Mr. Goodwin. My brother has Carl Drew, and Anita Prince, and Emmy Thorne—and me, if I count. But now trouble has come. The trouble is a woman—a woman named Bianca Voss."

Wolfe made a face. She said it and responded to it. "No, not an *affaire d'amour*, I'm sure of that. Though my brother has never married, I am certain this Bianca Voss has not attracted him that way. She first came there a little more than a year ago. My brother had told us to expect her, but we don't know where he had met her or where she came from. He designed a dress and a suit for her, and they were made there in the shop, but no bill was ever sent her. Then he gave her one of the rooms, the offices, on the third floor, and she started to come every day, and soon the trouble began. My brother never told us she had any authority, but she took it and he allowed her to. Sometimes she interferes directly, and sometimes through him. She pokes her nose into everything. She got my brother to discharge a fitter, a very capable woman, who had been with him for years. She has a private telephone line in her office upstairs, but no one else has. About two months ago some of the others persuaded me to try to find out about her, what her standing is, and I asked my brother, but he wouldn't tell me. I begged him to, but he wouldn't."

"It sounds," Wolfe said, "as if she owns the business. Perhaps she bought it."

Flora shook her head. "No, she hasn't. I'm sure she hasn't. She wasn't one of the financial backers in 1953, and since then there have been good profits, and anyway, my brother has control. But now she's going to cheapen it and spoil it, and he's going to let her, we don't know why. She wants him to design a factory line to be promoted by a chain of department stores using his name. She wants him to sponsor a line of Alec Gallant cosmetics on a royalty basis. And other things. We're against all of them, and my brother is, too, really, but we think he's going to give in to her, and that will ruin it."

She stopped to swallow. "Mr. Wolfe, I want you to ruin her."

He grunted. "By wiggling a finger?"

"No, but you can. I'm sure you can. I'm sure she has some hold on him, but I don't know what. I don't know who she is or where she came from. I don't know if Bianca Voss is her real name. She speaks with an accent, and it may be French, but if it is, it's from some part of France I don't know; I'm not sure what it is. I don't know when she came to America; she may be here illegally. She may have known my brother in France during the war; I was young then. You can find out. If she has a hold on my brother, you can find out what it is. If she is blackmailing him, isn't that against the law? Wouldn't that ruin her?"

"It might. It might ruin him too."

"Not unless you betrayed him." She gave a little gasp and added hastily, "I don't mean that, I only mean I am trusting you, you said I could, and you could make her stop, and that's all you would have to do. Couldn't you do just that?"

"Conceivably." Wolfe wasn't enthusiastic. "I fear, madam, that you're biting off more than you can chew. The procedure you suggest would be prolonged, laborious, and extremely expensive. It would probably require elaborate investigation abroad. Aside from my fee, which would not be modest, the outlay would be considerable and the outcome highly uncertain. Are you in a position to undertake it?"

"I am not rich myself, Mr. Wolfe. I have some savings. But my brother—if you get her away, if you release him from her—he is truly *généreux*—pardon—he is a generous man. He is not stingy."

"But he isn't hiring me, and your assumption that she is coercing him may be groundless." Wolfe shook his head. "No. Not a reasonable venture. Unless, of course, your brother himself consults me. If you care to bring him? Or send him?"

"Oh, I couldn't!" She waved it away. "You must see that isn't possible! When I asked him about her, I told you, he wouldn't tell me anything. He was annoyed. He is never abrupt with me, but he was then. I assure you, Mr. Wolfe, she is a villain. You are *sagace*—pardon—you are an acute man. You would know it if you saw her, spoke with her."

"Perhaps," Wolfe was losing patience. "Even so, my perception of her villainy wouldn't avail. No, madam."

"But you would know I am right." She opened her bag, fingered in it with both hands, came out with something, left her chair to step to Wolfe's desk, and put the something on the desk pad in front of him.

"There," she said, "that is three hundred dollars. For you that is nothing, but it shows how I am in earnest." She returned to the chair. "I know you never leave your home on business, you wouldn't go there, and I can't ask her to come here so you can speak with her, she would merely laugh at me, but you can. You can tell her you have been asked in confidence to discuss a matter with her and ask her to come to see you. You will not tell her what it is. She will come—she will be afraid not to—and that alone will show you she has a secret, perhaps many secrets. Then, when she comes, you will ask her whatever occurs to you. For that you do not need my suggestions. You are *sagace*."

"Pfui," Wolfe shook his head. "Everybody has secrets; not necessarily guilty ones."

"Yes," she agreed, "but not secrets that would make them afraid not to come to see Nero Wolfe. When she comes and you have spoken with her, we shall see. That may be all or it may not. We shall see."

I do not say that the three hundred bucks there on his desk was no factor. Even though income tax would take two thirds of it, there would be enough left for three weeks' supply of beer or for two days' salary for me. Another factor was plain curiosity: would Bianca Voss come or wouldn't she? Another was the chance that it might develop into a decent fee. Still another was her saying "We shall see" instead of "We'll see" or "We will see." He will always stretch a point, within reason, for people who use words as he thinks they should be used. But all of those together might not have swung him if he hadn't known that if he turned her down, and she went, I was pigheaded enough to go with her on leave of absence.

So he muttered at her, "Where is she?"

"At my brother's place. She always is."

"Give Mr. Goodwin the phone number."

"I'll get it. She may be downstairs." She got up and started for the phone on Wolfe's desk, but I told her to use mine and left my chair, and she came and sat, lifted the receiver, and dialed. In a moment she spoke. "Doris? Flora. Is Miss Voss around? . . . Oh. I thought she might have come down. . . . No, don't bother; I'll ring her private line."

She pushed the button down, told us, "She's up in her office," waited a moment, released the button, and dialed again. When she spoke, it was with another voice, as she barely moved her lips and brought it out through her nose, "Miss Bianca Voss? Hold the line, please. Mr. Nero Wolfe wishes to speak with you. . . . Nero Wolfe, the private detective."

She looked at Wolfe and he got at his phone. Having my own share of curiosity, I extended a hand for my receiver, and she let me take it and left my chair. As I got it to my ear Wolfe was speaking.

"This is Nero Wolfe. Is this Miss Bianca Voss?"

"Yes." It was more like "Yiss." "What do you want?" The "*wh*" and the "*w*" were way off.

"If my name is unknown to you, I should explain—"

"I know your name. What do you want?"

"I wish to invite you to call on me at my office. I have been asked to discuss certain matters with you, and—"

"Who asked you?"

"I am not at liberty to say. I shall—"

"*What kind of matters?*" The "*wh*" was more off.

"If you will let me finish. The matters are personal and confidential and concern you closely. That's all I can say on the telephone. I assure you that you would be ill-advised—"

A snort stopped him—a snort that might be spelled "Tzchaahh!" Followed by: "I know your name, yes! You are scum, I know, in your stinking sewer! Your slimy little ego in your big gob of fat! And you dare to—owul-gghh!"

That's the best I can do at reporting it. It was part scream, part groan, and part just noise. It was followed immediately by another noise, a mixture of crash and clatter, then others, faint rustlings, and then nothing.

I spoke to my transmitter: "Hello, hello, hello. Hello! Hello?"

I cradled it, and so did Wolfe. Flora Gallant was asking. "What is it? She hung up?" We ignored her. Wolfe said, "Archie? You heard."

"Yes, sir. So did you. If you want a guess, something hit her and she dragged the phone along as she went down and it struck the floor. The other noises, not even a guess, except that at the end she put the receiver back on and cut the connection or someone else did. It could be—"

Flora had grabbed my sleeve with both hands and was demanding. "What is it? What happened?"

I put a hand on her shoulder and made it emphatic: "I don't know what happened. There was a collection of sounds. You heard what I told Mr. Wolfe. Apparently something fell on her and then hung up the phone."

"But it couldn't! It is not possible!"

"That's what it sounded like. What's the number? The one downstairs."

She just gawked at me. I looked at Wolfe and he gave me a nod, and I jerked my arm loose, sat at my desk, got the Manhattan book, flipped to the G's and got the number, PL2–0330, and dialed it.

A refined female voice came, "Alec Gallant, Incorporated."

"This is a friend of Miss Voss," I told her. "I was just speaking to her on the phone, on her private line, and from the sounds I got, I think something may have happened to her. Will you send someone up to see? Right away. I'll hold the wire."

"Who is this speaking, please?"

"Never mind that. Step on it. She may be hurt."

I heard her calling to someone: then apparently she covered the transmitter. I sat and waited. Wolfe sat and scowled at me. Flora stood for some minutes at my elbow, staring down at me, then turned and went to the red leather chair and lowered herself onto its edge. I looked at my wristwatch: 11:40. It had said 11:31 when the connection with Bianca Voss had been cut.

More waiting, and then a male voice came: "Hello?"

"This is Carl Drew. What is your name please?"

"My name is Watson—John H. Watson. Is Miss Voss all right?"

"May I have your address, Mr. Watson?"

"Miss Voss knows my address. Is she all right?"

"I must have your address, Mr. Watson. I must insist. You will understand the necessity when I tell you that Miss Voss is dead. She was assaulted in her office and is dead. Apparently, from what you said, the assault came while she was on the phone with you, and I want your address. I must insist."

"Who assaulted her?"

"I don't know. Damn it, how do I know? I must—"

I hung up, gently not to be rude, swiveled and asked Flora, "Who is Carl Drew?"

"My brother's business manager. What happened?"

I looked at Wolfe. "My guess was close. Miss Voss is dead. In her office. He said she was assaulted, but he didn't say with what or by whom."

He glowered at me, then turned to let her have it. She was coming up from the chair, slow and stiff. When she was erect, she said, "No. No! It isn't possible!"

"I'm only quoting Carl Drew," I told her.

"But it's crazy! He said she is dead? Bianca Voss?"

"Distinctly." She looked as if she might be needing a prop, and I stood up.

"But how—" She let it hang. She repeated, "But how—" stopped again, turned, and was going.

When Wolfe called to her, "Here, Miss Gallant, your money!" she paid no attention, but kept on, and he poked it at me, and I took it and headed for the hall.

I caught up with her halfway to the front door, but when I offered it, she just kept going so I blocked her off, took her bag, opened it, dropped the bills in, closed it and handed it back.

I spoke. "Easy does it, Finger. Take a breath. Going without your stole?"

"Oh." She swallowed. "Where is it?" I got it for her.

"In my opinion," I said, "you need a little chivalry. I'll come and get you in a taxi."

She shook her head. "I'm all right."

"You are not. You'll get run over."

"No, I won't. Don't come. Just let me . . . please."

She meant it, so I stepped to the door and pulled it open, and she crossed the sill. I stood there and watched, thinking she might stumble going down the steps of the stoop, but she made it to the sidewalk and turned west toward Tenth Avenue. Evidently she wasn't completely paralyzed, since Tenth was one-way uptown.

There are alternative explanations for the fact that I did not choose to return immediately to the office. One would be that I was afraid to face the music—not the way to put it, since the sounds that come from Wolfe when he is good and sore are not musical. The other would be that purely out of consideration for him I decided he would rather be alone for a while. I prefer the latter. Anyway, I made for the stairs, but I was only halfway up the first flight when his bellow came, "Archie! Come here!"

I about-faced, descended, crossed the hall and stood on the threshold. "Yes, sir? I was going up to my room to see if I left the faucet dripping."

"Let it drip. Sit down."

I went to my chair and sat down. "Too bad," I said regretfully. "Three hundred dollars may be hay, but—"

"Shut up."

I lifted my shoulders half an inch and dropped them. He leaned back comfortably and eyed me.

"I must compliment you," he said, "on the ingenuity of your stratagem. Getting me with you on the phone, so that I could corroborate your claim that both you and Miss Gallant were here in my office at the moment the murder was committed was well conceived and admirably executed. But I fear it was more impetuous than prudent. You are probably in mortal jeopardy, and I confess I shall be seriously inconvenienced if I lose your services, even though you get only a long term in prison. So I would like to help, if I can. It will be obvious, even to a slower wit than Mr. Cramer's, that you and Miss Gallant arranged for the attack to occur on schedule, precisely at the moment that Miss Voss was speaking to me on the phone; and therefore, patently, that you were in collusion with the attacker. So our problem is not how to fend suspicion from you, but whether you can wriggle out of it, and if so how. No doubt you have considered it?"

"Yeah. Sure."

"And?"

"I think it's hopeless. I'm in for it. Not a prison term; I'll get six thousand volts. I know it will inconvenience you, but it will inconvenience me too. I regret it very much because it has been a rare experience working for you." I uncrossed my legs. "Look. Naturally, you are boiling. I let her come here, yes. I—uh—persuaded you to see her, yes. If you're in a tantrum, O.K., go ahead and tantrum and get it over with."

"I am not in a tantrum and 'tantrum' is not a verb."

"Then I take it back. Apparently it's worse than a tantrum, since instead of ragging me, you burlesque it. Can't you just tell me what you think of me?"

"No. It's not in my vocabulary. You realize what we are in for?"

"Certainly. If it was murder, and evidently it was, Flora Gallant will tell them where she was and what happened. Then we will have visitors, and not only that, but if and when someone is nominated for it and put on trial, we will be star witnesses because we heard it happen. Not eyewitnesses, earwitnesses. We can time it right to the minute. You will sit for hours on a hard wooden bench in a courtroom, with no client and no fee in sight. I know how you feel and I don't blame you. Go ahead and tell me what you think of me."

"You admit you are answerable?"

"No. I was unlucky."

"That doesn't absolve you. A man is as responsible for his luck as for his judgment. How long have you known that woman?"

"Nineteen hours. She picked me up on Thirty-eighth Street at five o'clock yesterday afternoon."

"Picked you up?"

"Yes. I thought she was tailing Putz, but she said she was after me. That gave me a sense of well-being and stimulated my manhood. I took her to a bar and bought her a drink—she took vermouth—and it came out that it was you she was really after. Thinking there might be a fee in it, I took her to a place and fed her and danced with her. If it had led to a fee, that would have gone on my expense account, but now I don't suppose—"

"No."

"Very well. She didn't tell me the whole story, but enough so it seemed possible it was worth half an hour of your time, and I told her to come at eleven this morning."

"How long were you out?"

"Until midnight. Altogether, seven hours."

"Did you take her home?"

"No. She was against it. I put her in a taxi."

"Did she phone you this morning before she came?"

"No."

"How did she come? In a cab?"

"I don't know. Fritz may know; he let her in."

"She probably did." His lips tightened. He released them. "Cabs and cars have thousands of accidents every day. Why couldn't hers have been one of them?" He came forward in the chair and rang for beer. "Confound it. It will save time and harassment if we have a report ready. You will type one. Your meeting with her yesterday, your conversation with her, and what occurred here today, including everything that was said. We will both sign it."

"Not everything that was said last evening."

"No, I suppose not. You said you got sentimental. What I sign I read, and I certainly wouldn't read that."

I swiveled and pulled the typewriter around and got out paper and carbons. Reports, especially when they are to be signed statements, have to be in triplicate.

That kept me busy the rest of the day, with an hour out for lunch and various interruptions, mostly phone calls, including one from Lon Cohen, of the *Gazette*, to ask for the low-down on the murder of Bianca Voss. I wondered why the cops had been so free and fast about Flora Gallant's call on Nero Wolfe, but that wasn't it: one of the *Gazette's* journalists had seen me at Colonna's with her, and Lon is one of a slew of people who have the idea that whenever I am seen anywhere near anybody who is anyhow connected with a death by violence, Nero Wolfe is looming. I told him our only interest in the Voss murder was not to get involved in it, which was no lie.

Over the years I have reported hundreds of long conversations to Wolfe, verbatim, some after a week or more had passed, and that typing job was no strain on my memory, but I took my time because I had to be darned sure of it, since he was going to sign it. Also he was going to read it, and in his present mood he would be delighted to tell me that he had not said "prolonged, difficult, and extremely expensive." He had said "prolonged, laborious, and extremely expensive." And I would have to retype a whole page.

So I took my time, and was on the last paragraph when he came down to the office from his afternoon session in the plant rooms, which is from four to six. When he had got settled at his desk I gave him the first five pages and he started reading. Back at the typewriter, I shot a glance at him now and then, and saw that his frown was merely normal. Finished, I took him the remainder, returned to my desk to arrange the carbons, and then got up to shake down my pants legs and stretch.

He is a fast reader. When he got to the end he cleared his throat. "One thing. Did I say 'not necessarily guilty ones'? Didn't I say 'not always guilty ones'?"

"No, sir. As you know, you like the word 'necessarily.' You like the way you say it. You may remember—"

The doorbell rang. I went to the hall, flipped the switch of the stoop light, and took a look through the one-way glass panel of the front door. It wasn't necessary to go closer to recognize Inspector Cramer, of Homicide.

II

I stepped into the office and told Wolfe, "Him." He compressed his lips and took in air through his nose.

"I see you've signed the statement," I said. "Shall I open the door a crack and slip it through to him and tell him that covers it and give him your regards?"

"No. A crack is open both ways. If he has a warrant for you, he could slip that through to you. Let him in."

I wheeled, walked to the front door, swung it wide, and made it hearty, "Just the man we wanted to see, Inspector Cramer! Do come in."

He was already in. By the time I had shut the door and turned around he had shed his hat and coat and dropped them on a chair, and by the time I had put the hat on the shelf where he knew darned well it belonged, and the coat on a hanger, and got to the office, he was already in the red leather chair and talking.

". . . and don't tell me you didn't know a crime had been committed or any of that tripe, and you had firsthand knowledge of it, both you and Goodwin, and do you come forward with it? No. You sit here at your desk and to hell with the law and the city of New York and your obligations as a citizen and a licensed private detective, and you—"

Wolfe had his eyes closed. I, back at my desk, had mine open. I always enjoy seeing Inspector Cramer worked up. He is big and brawny to start with, and then he seems to be expanding all over, and his round red face gets gradually redder, bringing out its contrast with his gray hair.

When he stopped for breath, Wolfe opened his eyes. "I assure you, Mr. Cramer, this is uncalled for. Mr. Goodwin has indeed been sitting here, but not idly. He has been fulfilling our obligations, his and mine, as citizens and licensed private detectives." He lifted sheets of paper. "This is a statement, signed by both of us. After you have read it, we'll answer questions if they're relevant."

Cramer didn't move, and Wolfe wouldn't, so I arose and got the statement and took it to Cramer. He snatched it from me, no thanks, glared at Wolfe, glanced at the heading on the first page, glared at me as I sat, and started to read. First he skimmed through it, and then went back and really read it. Wolfe was leaning back with his eyes closed. I passed the time taking in the changes of expression on Cramer's face. When he reached the end he turned back to one of the earlier pages for another look, and then aimed his sharp gray eyes at Wolfe.

"So you had it ready," he said, not with gratitude.

Wolfe opened his eyes and nodded. "I thought it would save time and trouble."

"Yeah. You're always thoughtful. I admit it agrees pretty well with Flora Gallant's story, but why shouldn't it? Is she your client?"

"Pfui. That statement makes it quite clear that I have no client."

"It does if it's all here. Did you leave anything out?"

"Yes. Much of Mr. Goodwin's conversation with Miss Gallant last evening. Nothing pertinent."

"Well, we'll want to study it. Of course some details are vitally important—for instance, that it was exactly eleven-thirty-one when you heard the blow."

Wolfe objected. "We heard no blow, identifiably. The statement does not say that we heard a blow."

Cramer found the place on page 9 and consulted it. "O.K. You heard a groan and a crash and rustles. But there was a blow. She was hit in the back of the head with a chunk of marble, a paperweight, and then a scarf was tied around her throat to stop her breathing. You say here at eleven-thirty-one."

I corrected him. "Not when we heard the groan. After that there were the other noises, then the connection went, and I said hello a few times, which was human but dumb. It was when I hung up that I looked at my watch and saw eleven-thirty-one. The groan had been maybe a minute earlier, say eleven-thirty. If a minute is important."

"It isn't. But you didn't hear the blow?"

"Not to recognize it as a blow, no."

He went back to the statement, frowning at it, reading parts of some pages and just glancing at others. He looked up at Wolfe. "I know how good you are at arranging words. This implies that Flora Gallant was a complete stranger to you, that you had never had anything to do with her or her brother or any of the people at that place, but it doesn't say so in so many words. I'd like to know."

"The implication is valid," Wolfe told him. "Except as related in that statement, I have never had any association with Miss Gallant or her brother or, to my knowledge, with any of their colleagues. Nor has Mr. Goodwin. . . . Archie?"

"Right," I agreed.

"I'll accept that for now." Cramer folded the statement and put it in his pocket. "Then you had never heard Bianca Voss' voice before and you couldn't recognize it on the phone?"

"Of course not."

"And you can't hear it now, since she's dead. So you can't swear it was her talking to you."

"Obviously."

"And that raises a point. If it was her talking to you, she was killed at exactly half past eleven. Now there are four important people in the organization who had it in for Bianca Voss. They have admitted it. Besides Flora Gallant, there is Anita Prince, fitter and designer, been with Gallant eight years; Emmy Thorne in charge of contacts and promotion, been with him four years; and Carl Drew, business manager, been with him five years. None of them killed Bianca Voss at half past eleven. From eleven-fifteen on, until the call came from Goodwin calling himself John H. Watson, Carl Drew was down on the main floor, constantly in view of four people, two of them customers. From eleven o'clock on, Anita Prince was on the top floor, the workshop, with Alec Gallant and two models and a dozen employees. At eleven-twenty Emmy Thorne called on a man by appointment at his office on Forty-sixth Street, and was with him and two other men until a quarter to twelve. And Flora Gallant was here with you. All airtight."

"Very neat," Wolfe agreed.

"Too damn neat. Of course there may be others who wanted Bianca Voss out of the way, but as it stands now, those four are out in front. And they're all—"

"Why not five? Alec Gallant himself?"

"All right, make it five. They're all in the clear, including him, if she was killed at eleven-thirty. So suppose she wasn't. Suppose she was killed earlier—half an hour or so earlier. Suppose when Flora Gallant phoned her from here and put you on to talk with her, it wasn't her at all, it was someone else imitating her voice, and she pulled that stunt, the groan and the other noises, to make you think you had heard the murder at that time."

Wolfe's brows were up. "With the corpse there on the floor?"

"Certainly."

"Then you're not much better off. Who did the impersonation? Their alibis still hold for eleven-thirty."

"I realize that. But there were nineteen women around there altogether, and a woman who wouldn't commit a murder might be willing to help cover up after someone else had committed it. You know that."

Wolfe wasn't impressed. "It's very tricky, Mr. Cramer. If you are supposing Flora Gallant killed her, it was elaborately planned. It wasn't until late last evening that Miss Gallant persuaded Mr. Goodwin to make an appointment for her here for eleven this morning. Did she kill Miss Voss, station someone there beside the corpse to answer the phone, rush down here and maneuver me into ringing Miss Voss' number? It seems a little farfetched."

"I didn't say it was Flora Gallant." Cramer hung on. "It could have been any of them. He or she didn't have to know she was going to come to see you and get you to ring that number. His plan might have been to ring it himself, before witnesses, to establish the time of the murder, and when your call came, whoever it was there by the phone got rattled and went ahead with the act. There are a dozen different ways it could have happened. Hell, I know it's tricky. I'm not asking you to work your brain on it. You must know why I brought it up."

Wolfe nodded. "Yes, I think I do. You want me to consider what I heard—and Mr. Goodwin. You want to know if we are satisfied that those sounds were authentic. You want to know if we will concede that they might have been bogus."

"That's it. Exactly."

Wolfe rubbed his nose with a knuckle, closing his eyes. In a moment he opened them. "I'm afraid I can't help you, Mr. Cramer. If they were bogus, they were well executed. At the time, hearing them, I had no suspicion that it was flummery. Naturally, as soon as I learned that they served to fix the precise moment of